OUR FOREVER MOMENT

The McCormicks
Book 7

ELENA AITKEN

Chapter One

MAUREEN

Present

CROWS' feet. Laugh lines. *Salt-and-pepper* strands.

Such silly names meant to soften the blow of getting older.

All they did was make me shake my head. Or sigh. It depended on the day.

Today, I sighed.

I took one last look in the mirror and tried to stifle my groan. Maybe a facial or one of those peels that the younger girls were always going on about might have helped. But it was too late for that now. The reflection in the mirror was going to have to do.

Lines, wrinkles, spots, and all.

Never in all my fifty-six years had I given much thought to aging. I'd never been one to spend hundreds of dollars on fancy creams, or worry about dyeing the gray away. I'd always considered myself a fairly attractive woman, even as time began to take its toll.

1

But this was different.

Very different.

I hadn't seen Adam since I was a girl.

Yes. It was *very* different.

I reached for the makeup bag Jade, my daughter-in-law, had helped me pack just for the occasion. At my request, Jade, who had a lot more experience with this type of thing, had helped me pick out a few flattering shades of eyeshadow and even a new lipstick.

I pulled out the tube of lipstick and leaned in close to the mirror. If there ever was going to be a time to try it out, it might as well be now. After all, what else did I have to lose? My sons—most of them, anyway—thought I was crazy, traveling across the continent to a remote mountain inn in the North Carolina Mountains, only a few days before Christmas to meet a man who was a virtual stranger.

And maybe I was.

I laughed at myself as I pressed the tube to my lip. Right as my hotel room plunged into darkness.

My breath caught in my throat and panic gripped me.

"Calm down, Maureen." My voice was loud in the dark, empty room. "It's just a power outage." I laughed at myself and shook my head. I'd lived through many power outages over the years. Especially as a girl when I spent my summers in the mountainous town of Cedar Springs. Besides, I was a grown woman. There was nothing to be scared of.

Still. It *was* dark.

I'd arrived at the inn earlier in the afternoon, and even before the sun went down, it was dark and gloomy outside as the storm that had been threatening started to make good on its threats. It wasn't yet dinnertime, but with the thick storm clouds blocking out what little sunlight there might be left, my room was shockingly dark. And when, after a few minutes, the power didn't return, I fumbled for my purse and made my way out of the room and down to the main lobby of the inn.

I made the right choice. Candles were lit among the pine boughs that seemed to be draped on every free surface for the Christmas season. And paired with the welcoming glow from the huge fireplace, it was easy to forget that there was a power outage at all since the scene was so festive.

"Not to worry, Mrs. McCormick." Lucy Gibbons, the innkeeper who'd greeted me earlier, appeared beside me. She set a light hand on my shoulder. "It's not unusual for the power to go out in such a heavy storm, but we do have backup generators, and they should be up and going any minute now."

"Oh, I'm not worried." I smiled warmly and let my gaze drift around the room. "It's absolutely beautiful in here."

The woman beamed with pride. "Christmas is my favorite holiday and there's nothing quite as romantic as the festive season in the mountains, is there?" She winked, and I blushed despite the fact that Lucy couldn't have known why I was in North Carolina at the Merry Falls Inn less than a week before Christmas, or who I was meeting. "And now, with the snow coming down so heavily, it looks as if we'll be snowed in."

"Snowed in?" I turned my head around to face her. "The road is closed?"

Lucy nodded. "I just got word. The mountains are so unpredictable and although it doesn't happen terribly often, it does happen that sometimes the plows just can't keep up and—"

"But if the road is closed..." *Would Adam be able to get through?* I didn't finish the thought aloud.

"Not to worry, Mrs. McCormick. They'll have them cleared before Christmas."

Christmas? I hadn't even thought of that. My boys would kill me if I wasn't back in time for the holidays. They really wouldn't be happy if I was trapped.

But that wasn't my primary concern at the moment.

If Adam couldn't make it, after all these years and all our careful planning...well, I didn't want to think about the idea that my sons had been right, and it was a foolish idea coming so far for a man I hadn't seen in almost forty years.

Most of my sons. Declan had not only been supportive but had taken it upon himself to locate Adam as a special Christmas surprise a year earlier. I'd dedicated my life to my boys and after my husband's betrayal, when my eldest was only eighteen, I had shut my heart off to the idea of ever loving again.

But time had a way of softening things. And after I'd witnessed the way each of my sons had found their partners and a happiness I'd never seen in them before, I couldn't help but start to believe that maybe love might exist after all. And then, when my *daughters*, who really weren't my daughters at all, but my sons' half-sisters—a complicated relationship if ever there was one—also found their happiness, I was convinced that it wasn't necessarily too late.

I looked around the festive inn. *Maybe Adam had made it? Maybe it wasn't too late after all.*

"What about tonight?" I reached a hand out and stopped the busy innkeeper before she could run off. "Will anyone be able to get through the roads tonight?"

The look on the other woman's face told me everything I needed to know, but it wasn't until Lucy shook her head that my heart fell.

"With a heavy snowfall like this, it can be pretty dangerous on those mountain roads. If anyone was out there, they prob-ably would have been turned around before they closed the gates. But—"

"Ms. Gibbons?" A rather frazzled-looking young man tapped on the innkeeper's shoulder and shot me an apologetic look. "I really am sorry to interrupt," he said. "But there's a bit of a…" He leaned in and tried to whisper. "Situation."

"A situation?"

"Is everything okay?" I straightened my shoulders and immediately went into problem-solving mode. As a mother of four boys, it was a mode I was proficient in. "If there's anything I can do, please let me know. I can—"

"Oh no." Lucy offered me a warm smile. "Everything is just fine. And like I said, the backup power should be on any moment now. There's fresh coffee, tea, or hot chocolate over by the fire. The restaurant is open and the bar next door is also available for meals and, of course, libations to get you through the cold night. The band will be—"

"The Lost Ridge Ramblers are great," the young man interjected.

"They really are." Lucy nodded. "It should all be quite festive and fun."

"It does sound fun." The innkeeper was busy, and I didn't want to add to her stress by inquiring about Adam's arrival status. I glanced out a nearby window into the snowy night and the quickly accumulating drifts, and sighed.

I didn't need anyone to tell me what I already knew.

Adam wasn't coming.

"Don't let me keep you." I forced a smile. "I think I'll help myself to a tea and sit by the fire for a while. It's really quite beautiful in here."

Lucy beamed. "Thank you. We take pride in our holiday decorations."

"It shows." I made my way to the beverage cart where, instead of the tea, I opted for a hot chocolate with marshmallows in it. I probably wouldn't be able to sleep due to the sugar, but given the storm, sleep was likely off the table anyway.

Two inviting chairs were set in front of the fireplace. One

was occupied by an elderly lady working on a crochet project. The other was free.

"Is this seat taken?"

The woman looked up from her project and tipped her head. "It is now." She nodded toward the chair and set the crochet project down in her lap. "Is that hot chocolate you're drinking?"

"It is." I looked from my hot drink to the woman. "Would you like a cup?"

"With extra marshmallows, if you don't mind."

I grinned. "I'll be right back."

I returned a moment later with a mug for my new friend, complete with the requested extra marshmallows.

"Don't tell my niece." The woman winked as she accepted the cup. "She means well, but she's very bossy."

A small chuckle slipped from me as I took my seat. "I have the same problem with my sons. They're not too bad, yet," I added quickly with a shake of my head. "But if they knew about this storm…well, I can't even imagine what they'd say. They didn't like me coming so close to Christmas as it was."

"Well, what they don't know won't hurt them, will it?" The older woman lifted her mug in a toast. "My name is Elise, and I don't think there's anything wrong with keeping a few harmless secrets from our children."

"It's very nice to meet you, Elise. I'm Maureen." I grinned over the rim of my cup. "And I couldn't agree more."

I had kept more than my share of secrets from my children over the years. It was what mothers did. But only when it really mattered. For example, children had no business knowing the sins of their father. It was the mother's job to protect her children. And that's exactly what I'd done. For as long as I could.

Despite what others thought, I'd long known about Harold's affair and the children borne from it. I'd never forget the day I'd discovered the photograph in his briefcase of the two little girls. They looked to be about the same ages as my two youngest boys, Declan and Cal, and I'd known at once exactly what it meant. The girls shared the same beautiful eyes as my own boys, along with their father's nose. There was no doubt whose children they were.

He hadn't taken great pains to hide it from me, but at the same time, he behaved as if everything were normal. Maybe I should have confronted him years earlier, but for reasons that were my own, I never could bring myself to say anything.

What would have been the point?

They had a nice marriage. Harold was a good provider. A good father. He loved me, and I loved him. It didn't matter that we weren't *in* love. In college, there'd been a time when Harold had been desperately in love with me. His pursuit was relentless. He showered me with gifts and compliments and finally, when I'd run out of reasons to object, I found myself loving him back. It wasn't a passionate, couldn't quite breathe, love. But it was enough.

At least, I thought it was.

And it had been enough for a little while. It wasn't long after Mitch, my second son, was born that I started to notice a shift in Harold. It was also about then when I had two toddlers in tow that I'd started packing up the boys and spending summers at the lake in the house I'd frequented as a girl that my father had left me when he passed away. After a minor bout of the *baby blues* that lasted a little too long, I'd once more been drawn to the one place I'd fallen in love as a young woman.

I hadn't understood my feelings back then, not completely. But time and distance had made it perfectly clear. Cedar Springs was home. Harold was busy building his career in the city, but he found time to make the drive every weekend and join his young family in my happy place.

The mountains were healing, and I'd returned to the city in the fall rejuvenated, refreshed and pregnant with Declan.

It was also that summer that Harold had done some *healing* of his own, and unbeknownst to me at the time, found love with someone else as well.

For years, I kept the charade of a happy family. Every summer, I would retreat to the lake. It was the only place I felt complete, and—although I'd never admit it to anyone, especially myself—being at the lake connected me to a time when I'd been the happiest I'd ever been.

Harold would arrive on Friday evenings with a bottle of wine and a fresh bouquet of flowers from the greenhouse on the highway. He'd spend Saturday and Sunday with the boys on the water, pulling them behind the boat as they showed off their growing water-skiing and wakeboarding skills, or teaching them to fish. On cooler days, Harold would take the boys into the forest, where they'd hike for hours. He'd point out animal signs and show them how to build shelters and make fires. He loved his boys, and he was an excellent father.

And that's why I'd stayed quiet for so many years. It was more important for Ian, Mitch, Declan, and Cal to have a father who loved them present in their lives than it was for me to have a loving or faithful husband.

If I were honest, I'd always blamed myself in a way for Harold seeking love from someone else. Certainly, I loved Harold but I'd never loved him the way I knew I should have. I'd always held back.

How could I not, when I'd already given my heart away years earlier?

"This is delicious."

I was pulled from my memory and back into the moment as the woman seated across from me sipped at her drink.

"It really is." I tested my own drink and closed my eyes as the sweet, delicious chocolate coated my tongue. "Oh wow. It really is good." I opened my eyes to see Elise enjoying her drink the same way.

"Isn't it? They've always had the best hot chocolate here at Christmas. Maybe it's the spirit of the season that makes it taste so good."

"Maybe." I took another sip. "Or it could be the hint of peppermint."

Elise laughed, a sweet sound. She plucked a tiny marsh-mallow from the top and popped it in her mouth. "You're here on your own."

It wasn't a question, but something about the woman made me want to talk. "I'm actually supposed to be meeting some-one," I said. "But I don't think he's coming,"

Elise took a long, slow sip of her drink, and when she looked up again, there was chocolate on her upper lip. "Do you have a reason to think he might stand you up?"

I did. But at the same time, I didn't.

"Are you here with your niece?" I deftly changed the subject.

The older woman laughed before leaning forward and winking conspiratorially. "She'd...how do the kids say it now? *Freak out* if she knew I was down here by myself. I told her I was going to bed, and she had some work to do. She works too much. She tried to tell me that we couldn't come this year. But I insisted."

Elise's choice of words struck me, and I, too, laughed.

"This year? Do you come here a lot?"

The older woman's face softened. "Every single year for over sixty years."

"Really? Sixty?

"Sixty-one, to be specific."

"Wow." I sat up in my seat. "That must be a record. You've been a guest here for sixty-one years?"

Elise laughed. "Well, not quite a guest. At least not always. When I was a girl, much younger than I am now, I took a job here a few years out of high school. I started out cleaning rooms." She chuckled. "It was not a glamorous job by any stretch of the imagination, but for me, it was the greatest opportunity I could have been offered."

Fascinated, I settled back in my chair, the mug warming my hands as I listened.

"You see," Elise continued, "that was back in the days when there weren't very many choices for unmarried girls. Or married ones, for that matter," she added as an afterthought. "Not unless your family had a lot of money. And mine did not. It would have been different for you. I must have at least forty years on you."

"I'll be fifty-six next year."

"Ah, I just celebrated eighty-eight. Those years make quite a difference."

I couldn't argue with that. I'd often thought of my own mother, for whom going to college had never even been an option. I was also very much aware that I'd been born to a father who was a physician and, as such, had enjoyed a certain level of privilege.

"I'd grown up poor in a little town north of here with fewer opportunities than there were people. So when I heard that Merry Falls Inn was hiring, it felt very exotic, like an adventure. And I was more than ready for a little adventure."

I couldn't miss the sparkle in the woman's eye as she spoke about the past.

"That must have been so exciting, Elise. What an adventure, indeed. This place must have made quite an impact on you if you kept coming back for all these years."

Elise took her time looking around the lobby, a warm smile on her face as she took it all in. "I sure didn't know all those years ago how much of a mark on my life it would leave. That's for sure." She was quiet for a moment and then, as if she realized I was still there, she shook her head clear. "I fell in love."

I waited a beat. "With Merry Falls Inn? Or with someone else?"

The smile on Elise's face told me the answer, even before she spoke. "Both."

I knew that feeling well. I smiled to myself a little, gave myself a moment to pull up the memory and started to share my story.

Thirty-Seven Years Ago...

I was in love. Totally and completely in love. There was no other word for the way I felt. I could feel it in my bones and every breath that I took when I looked out, off the deck at the lake below. I was totally in love with Cedar Springs and the mountain lake.

My father bought the cabin when I was a child and had started taking me and my older sister to the lake for the summers, almost as long as I could remember. But what I couldn't remember was ever feeling the way I felt at that exact moment. I attributed it to the fact that I was no longer a child.

Freshly graduated from high school, and at the very mature age of eighteen, I was a woman. I looked at things differently now. With an eye of maturity. Which was why when I looked out off the deck that towered over the blue, mountain lake where I'd spent my childhood summers swimming and splashing, I saw that same view now with love in my eyes.

The footsteps on the deck boards behind me interrupted my quiet moment of reflection. A second later, my best friend Sue Ann appeared next to me. Sue Ann draped herself over the railing, her arms full of bangles, clacking against the wood.

"Isn't it amazing?" I continued to gaze out at the view.

"What?"

I turned to stare at my friend. "The view. The lake. This place. It's magical, don't you think?" With both hands on the rails, I tipped my head back and inhaled deeply.

"I think you've lost your mind." Sue Ann laughed. "It's the lake. The same lake it's been every summer since we were kids."

"Sue Ann!" I didn't bother hiding my exasperation. "We're not kids anymore."

"And?"

I sighed dramatically and rolled my eyes. "I've decided that it's time to grow up."

"We *are* growing up."

I spun to face my friend. "No. I mean like *really* grow up. It's time to get serious. No more little girl games. We need to start paying attention to the things that really matter in life."

Sue Ann scrunched up her nose and shrugged. "Like the view?"

"No, silly. Like *life.*" I held out my arms and spun around while my friend looked on in confusion. "I'm finally ready to understand what love feels like. And I *am* in love."

"With…"

"The lake." I was quickly growing impatient with my friend's complete lack of understanding. "This place. I feel it in my bones. This place is special."

Her friend raised her eyebrows in question, so I continued.

"And now I want more. I want to feel the love of—"

"Don't say it." Sue Ann held up a hand. "Do *not* say a man."

"Why not?" I dropped my arms. "It's true. I'm done with boys. I'm ready for a man."

"You're done with boys?" My friend laughed. "How can you possibly be done with boys when you've never even had a boyfriend?"

Just because it was true didn't mean I wanted my best friend to point it out. Besides, Sue Ann was very quickly ruining my mood. I'd woken up on the first day of summer, ready to take on the world as a *woman*. Which, of course, meant I was going to need my best friend by my side. No one should be a woman on her own. Not when you were only eighteen.

"The reason I never had a boyfriend was because all the *boys* back home are just that—boys," I said matter-of-factly.

"I'm pretty sure there were men back home, too."

I ignored her. "Like I said. I'm ready for a *man*."

"Whatever." Sue Ann groaned. "I don't know about any *men*. But I'm sure hoping there are some cute boys at the dance tonight. I need you to help me pick which dress to wear. I have that black lace one that's just like the one Madonna wore. Or maybe the pink one. It's hot pink."

My earlier attempt at grown-up seriousness forgotten, I linked my arm through Sue Ann's and pulled my friend into the house and up to my bedroom, where we spent the afternoon trying on dresses, teasing our hair, dancing to Bananarama and dreaming about boys—or *men*—and giggling loud enough to earn more than one warning to be quiet from my mother before she finally kicked us out of the house altogether and sent us down to the lake to play.

As it turned out, as mature and serious as I'd been about

being in *love* with the place, I still wasn't too old to run and jump off the dock the same way I had every summer previously.

Chapter Two

Almost One Year Ago

New Year's Eve

"HAPPY NEW YEAR, MOM!" Cal, my youngest son, grabbed me around the waist and spun me around, causing me to shriek. "It's going to be a fabulous year, don't you think?"

I couldn't help but laugh. I scanned the room. I was surrounded by all four of my boys and their partners, all beautiful and kind women. Along with two pseudo daughters who I'd never expected. Amber and Chelsea were my sons half-sisters and my ex-husband's illegitimate daughters. I had spent far too long avoiding the young women who were a living reminder of my husband's betrayal for so many years.

It wasn't their fault that their father made poor life choices. It took some time, but once I'd gotten to know the girls properly, I could see what lovely young ladies they were, and it wasn't hard to welcome them into my life with open arms.

There was nothing but love and happiness surrounding me. I'd moved back to Cedar Springs, the mountain lake community that had always felt like home to me, and I had a grand-child on the way. What else could I want out of life?

"Yes," I answered Cal. "It's going to be an absolutely amazing year." I kissed my movie star son on the cheek. "Happy New Year, son."

His eyes sparkled. He reached an arm out and welcomed his girlfriend, Milena, into their little circle.

"Happy New Year, Mrs.— Maureen." The girl blushed and dipped her head a little. Her sweetness was a perfect complement to Cal. And judging by the way he looked at her, Cal couldn't agree more.

A voice behind them pulled my attention, and I was quickly led away for more New Year wishes from the rest of my family. Finally, I was able to extricate myself from the joyful crowd and retreat to a quiet corner, where I pulled the enve-lope out of my pocket.

I stared at the handwriting. It was somewhat shakier than my memory recalled, but that was to be expected. It had been almost forty years since I'd seen the still familiar handwriting. My hands trembled, the paper shaking.

Adam.

I hesitated and finally stuffed the envelope away again.

It's your turn, Mom, Declan had said when he handed me the envelope right before the clock struck midnight. Such a roman-tic, my second youngest child. I should have guessed that after I'd told Declan about my first love, he would find Adam for me. It was fitting, really…Declan reminded me so much of the young Adam I'd known—determined to save the world, even at the expense of themselves. Fortunately, Declan realized he didn't have to choose one over the other and had allowed himself to love.

Had Adam ever made the same realization?

When Declan was a boy, the summer he'd broken his leg and was unable to keep up with the rest of the boys, he'd spent a lot of time with me, sipping iced tea and eating ice cream on the deck looking out over the lake. I must have been feeling nostalgic that year when I'd told Declan all about Adam, the man I'd once known who'd left his home behind to *save the world*. Years later, I'd see firsthand the impact those stories had made on Declan when he followed suit and created his own charitable foundation.

But what I hadn't told him until very recently was that Adam had been my first love all those years ago, and after he left Cedar Springs, we'd never spoken again.

For almost forty years, Adam Lancaster had been nothing more than a fond memory and a *might have been*.

Until now.

Present

"Because we don't tell our children everything," Elise chimed in as I took a break from the story to sip my drink. "Smart woman."

"Well, I don't know about that." I set my mug down. "After all, I did finally tell him that Adam was my first love and it's because of that, and my son's huge heart and unlimited resources, that I'm here at all. Declan tracked him down and then, about a year ago, I got the letter. I guess that's when all this started." I waved my hand around vaguely before tucking it into my lap again.

"He does sound like a sweet boy."

"The sweetest." I loved all my sons equally. They'd all grown into good men, and I was proud of each of them. But Declan was truly the kindest, most giving man I'd ever met. He'd dedicated his life to charity and helping others. "What about you...do you have children?" I didn't want to monopolize the conversation. Besides, talking about something else would serve as a good distraction. "You mentioned a niece."

Elise nodded. "Susan. We're not actually related by blood. My best friend's girl." Her eyes lit up when she talked about her niece. "She's the closest thing I ever got to having children of my own, but she's like a daughter to me. There's something about being an auntie and not a mother that creates a special bond."

I wouldn't know. My older sister died in a car crash shortly after her twenty-first birthday before she ever had the chance to marry or have children of her own. Sue Ann ended up marrying, but she moved to the coast. Although they still kept in touch, I didn't know her children well. Still, I nodded, and Elise continued talking.

"We've always been close. Her own parents have been gone for years now, and her children are grown as well, so I guess I'm the perfect outlet for all of her worry."

Despite her tone, I could see how much Elise cared for her niece and valued that concern. "They only worry because they care."

Elise looked up and shook her head slightly. "It makes you wonder, doesn't it? When did the roles reverse exactly?"

I chuckled and nodded in complete understanding. "You said earlier that you fell in love with the inn and…"

"There was a special someone." Elise's gaze took on a faraway look. "I was so young and naive, I didn't even realize what I was feeling. It was my first time away from home, surrounded by new people. It was a heady feeling."

"I can't even imagine. It must have been very exciting."

Elise leaned her head back against the chair, her soft, white curls pillowed around her face. She closed her eyes and a smile slid over her lips as she lost herself in the memory. After a moment, she opened her eyes again and nodded, as if remembering that I was there. "It was very exciting indeed. The first time I met Alex, I was at a loss for words. I'm sure I stood there like a dullard, with my mouth just opening and closing. You see, Alex was the child of a very prominent businessman from town and ten years older."

"Ohh…forbidden love?"

The older woman's face clouded, and I immediately felt bad for making her talk at all. They sat in silence for a moment before Elise once more changed the subject.

"You said your son found Adam about a year ago. But that wasn't the start of the story, was it?"

I tilted my head, confused by the sudden switch in topics. "What do you mean?"

Elise leaned forward, her crochet project once more in her hands. "When you got the letter," she said again. "I don't think that was the start of anything." There was a sparkle in her eye that made me chuckle. "I think it started long before that."

I was a clever woman, and she wasn't wrong. I hadn't spoken about Adam to anyone except Sue Ann and even then, that was a very long time ago. Yet, something about Elise made it easy to open up, and maybe it was past time to tell my story.

"I guess you're right," I admitted. "The story did start a long, long time ago. It feels like a lifetime ago. It's quite a long story, really."

"That works out then." The older woman licked her lips and grinned. "Because I have nothing but time on my hands."

Thirty-Seven Years Ago…

Everyone was excited about the summer solstice festival. It was the biggest party of the summer, or at least, it was the *first* party of the summer. Every summer since I'd been old enough to attend, I had counted down the days until I and my girlfriends would put on our prettiest dresses, often bought new for the occasion, spend hours doing one another's hair, and, arm and arm, would run down Main Street to the water's edge, where rows of booths were set up.

Food vendors sold everything from hot dogs to popcorn and lemonade. There were usually rows of handicrafts and locally grown vegetables and flowers, but my friends and I only gave them a cursory glance as we made our way to where the action was.

The dance floor.

"The band is *so* good. I don't know how I'm ever going to dance in this." Sue Ann had opted for the black lace dress that might not be at all like anything Madonna ever wore, but it was going to be very difficult to dance in. I was happy I'd opted for the denim skirt and white sleeveless blouse—with plenty of bracelets, of course.

"You'll be fine."

"Where there's a will, there's a way. Come on." Sue Ann pulled me toward the dance floor as soon as we got close enough. "Let's dance."

"With who?"

"With each other, silly." Sue Ann grabbed my hands and spun me around and around until we were both out of breath and laughing.

"Okay, okay." I pulled myself away from my friend. "I need a break. Let's go get a lemonade."

"You go." Sue Ann waved me away. "I'm not ready yet." Sue Ann grinned at me and danced her way toward a circle of girls we knew from *summer*s past as also being summer kids.

During the summer season, Cedar Springs was made up of two groups: the locals and the summers. I and my family fell into the latter group, having spent all of my summers since I'd been a small child in the big wooden house on the lake.

The two groups would mingle occasionally, but for the

most part, there were clear dividing lines, and it was unusual to see new faces in either group. But that didn't keep me from dreaming, the way teenage girls did, that this would be the summer a new, handsome young man would show up in town and sweep me off my feet.

I'd been dreaming especially hard this year, as I was newly graduated from high school and, as I'd tried to tell Sue Ann earlier, ready for a *man*. I'd had enough of the silly boys from home, and although I wouldn't turn down the prospect of a summer romance, my eye was on the fall, when I'd finally be able to leave home for college and start my adult life.

I watched Sue Ann and the other girls for a moment before turning away with a laugh and going in search of the lemonade stand.

"One please." I placed my order and began digging in my purse for the change to pay for my drink when an unfamiliar voice stopped me.

"Make it two."

My head snapped up and the words of protest I'd been planning to speak died on my lips as I stared into the deepest, greenest eyes I'd ever seen.

I stood unspeaking as the boy—no, the young man—handed over the money to pay for the drinks. He took a paper cup and handed it to me. It was only then that I found my voice once again. "I can pay for my own drinks."

"I have no doubt you can."

I looked at the refreshment in my hand and back to the unfamiliar face.

"A simple thank-you would do." His eyes sparkled, and his lips twitched up into a grin.

I found myself smiling in return. "Thank you…"

"Adam." He extended his free hand. "It's nice to meet you…"

"Maureen." I put my hand in his, and immediately a flash

of heat shot through me. I'd only read about such things in the novels that I and Sue Ann would sneak from our mothers' nightstands. Never had I guessed such a thing existed in the real world.

I didn't release his grasp, but instead looked from our joined hands, up to his face and back to our hands.

"Maureen."

The way my name slipped from his lips mesmerized me. Or maybe it was the touch of his skin on mine. Or maybe it was just him. But I seemed to have the same effect on him. I didn't know how long we stood there staring at each other, but finally, someone jostled past us to get a drink, and the spell was broken.

My hand slipped from his, and we were forced apart. There was a moment of irrational panic, and then Adam was there, his hand lightly on my back. "Maybe we should get out of the way. It's a little quieter over there."

I let him lead me to an empty picnic table.

"I've never seen you here before," I said once we were seated facing each other. "Are you visiting?"

"I guess I am." He shrugged one shoulder. "I'm visiting my aunt and uncle for the summer before…well, I guess before I have to become an adult in the fall." He laughed.

It was such a rich, warm, welcoming sound that I found myself laughing along with him despite the fact that he looked very much like an adult already. I wasn't a great judge of age, but Adam was definitely at least a few years older than me.

"What happens in the fall?" I took a little sip of lemonade. "Are you headed to college?"

Adam shook his head. "I just graduated, actually."

I tipped my head and narrowed my eyes. "From high school?"

He laughed again. "From college."

I almost spat out my drink. "You've graduated from college already?"

He shrugged again; I was beginning to recognize the gesture as a way to deflect attention. "I recently finished my last exams in optometry school, actually."

"Wow. Optometry school?" I put both hands flat on the wooden table. "You mean, you're a doctor?"

"An optometrist, yes." Again, he shrugged. "Not officially, actually. I still need my exam results."

I could tell he was being modest and wasn't worried in any way about his exams. I lifted my cup. "A toast to you, then. Congratulations. I should be the one buying you the drink."

He met my cup with a cheers, and we each drank before he spoke again. "Maybe I'm old-fashioned, but I could never let such a pretty girl buy me a drink."

A blush heated my cheeks, and I had to look away.

"I also could never let another minute pass by without asking that very pretty girl if she would do me the honor of dancing with me."

My cheeks had to be flaming red, but there was no way I could not accept the offer. I looked up to see a goofy grin on his face.

"May I have this dance?"

I nodded, my heart racing as I took his hand and let him lead me onto the dance floor.

Present

"He must have been much older than you." Elise wiggled her eyebrows, and I couldn't help but giggle a little.

"He was." I nodded. "By almost seven years. But I didn't know that right away."

If Elise thought anything about the age gap, she didn't say anything, but I hadn't expected her to. Back then, an older boy dating a younger girl wasn't anything unusual. I was eighteen, a young woman capable of making my own decisions. And that summer, all my decisions revolved around Adam.

I once more scanned the room, as I had been all evening. There was still no sign of him. There was no sign of anyone new at the inn at all. While we'd been sitting by the fire, guests had come and gone, helping themselves to warm drinks and taking in the Christmas decorations on their way to the dining room. None of them seemed at all concerned by the worsening storm outside.

We sat in silence for a moment while I let the memories from that summer so long ago take over. I hadn't allowed myself the luxury of remembering those magical, heady weeks for so long…too long.

After the solstice dance, we were nearly inseparable. I would pack picnic baskets full of leftover fried chicken, deviled egg sandwiches, juicy strawberries, and of course, bottles of freshly squeezed lemonade for us to feast on as we lay on a blanket in a quiet corner of the beach, or in a grassy meadow, away from the crowds and my nosy friends.

I never could bring myself to drink lemonade after that summer.

"Excuse me, ladies."

Elise and I turned to see a young male employee with an armload of wood.

"If it's okay with you, I'll just be a moment stoking the fire."

"Thank you, Billy." Elise gave the boy a warm smile. "You take such good care of us."

"I do what I can, ma'am." They watched as he set about placing fresh logs in the fireplace. The wood snapped and crackled as it caught flame. "Is there anything else I can get either of you?" He glanced at their empty cups. "Some more hot chocolate, perhaps?"

"Oh, dear. I'll be up all night if I have any more."

"I'm afraid I'd be the same," I added, although I had a feeling I'd be up all night worried about Adam anyway.

"Actually, can you tell me if anyone else has checked in?"

Billy's lips pressed into a line, and he shook his head solemnly. "As far as I know, no one has made it through the storm at all. Is there anyone in particular you're waiting for, ma'am? I'll go check."

I hesitated to give Adam's name. If he'd made it through the storm, he'd already be there. Which meant he was either trapped in town at the bottom of the mountain, or he hadn't come at all. The last thought stung. *Surely he wouldn't stand me up? Not after so long? Not again?*

"No." I managed a small smile and a quick shake of my head. "That's fine. Thank you very much."

"If there's anything I can get either of you, please don't hesitate to ask, okay?"

We sent him off with assurances that we would in fact ask if we required anything.

"Such a nice young man." I watched him go. "He reminds me of—"

"Are you going to tell me, or not?"

I snapped my head around to refocus on my companion. "I'm sorry." I shook my head. "Tell you what?"

Elise lifted her eyes from her project. "Tell me what was in the letter, of course."

Almost One Year Ago

New Year's Day

It was half past one in the morning by the time I got home from the New Year's party. It was way past the time when I should have been in bed, but with the letter still unread, there was no way I'd be able to sleep.

I sat at the kitchen table and took a deep breath. I hadn't heard from Adam in over forty years. *Did he remember me?*

Obviously he had, if he'd bothered to write me a letter.

But *what* did he remember of me?

Did he remember that summer? The love we had for each other? Did he remember—

"Stop it, Maureen." My voice was sharp in the quiet condo.

There was no point in putting it off any longer. With shaking hands, I tore open the envelope and slid the paper free.

Dearest Maureen,

I'm not sure where to begin.

When your son reached out, to say that I was shocked would be an understatement.

I never thought I would have the chance to speak to you again, even through words on paper. I can't tell you what it means to have the opportunity.

I've thought about you so many times over the years. I wondered if you'd married. If you became the mother you so badly wanted to be. If you were happy.

Selfishly, I couldn't bring myself to ask after you. I think I was afraid of the answer. If you were happy, I would be devastated for myself. But if you were unhappy, I wouldn't be able to bear it.

Over time, I began to think of you only as a sweet memory that never failed to bring a smile to my face.

Life has been good to me, Maureen. I hope it has been equally good to you.

We've lived a lifetime apart and if there is one thing I've learned over the years, it is that our time on this earth is limited and I don't know about you, but I'm not getting any younger. So, with that in mind, I'm going to be bold.

I'd very much like to see you again, Maureen.

There is no rush as I will be overseas finishing my work for another year before returning to North America to stay.

I eagerly await your reply.

Yours always,

Adam

Chapter Three

Present

I FINISHED READING the letter aloud and folded it along the well-worn creases and set it in my lap. At this point, I'd read the letter so many times, I knew the contents by heart. But I liked seeing Adam's careful and precise handwriting and holding the paper he'd held in my hands. Despite the distance still between us, it made me feel more connected to him.

It should have felt strange sharing the details of our communication with a total stranger. I hadn't shared the letter in its entirety with anyone. Not even my children. Perhaps that's why they all thought I'd completely lost the plot by flying across the continent only days before Christmas.

I couldn't say what it was about Elise. But something about the older woman made it easy for me to open up.

"We wrote a few letters back and forth after that." I offered up the information before Elise could ask. "With his travels, it was often easier than to rely on technology, and honestly…it was kind of…"

"Romantic?" Elise grinned. "I'm not too old to recognize romance when I see it."

"I hope I'm never too old to recognize romance." I chuckled and returned her smile. "And it *was* romantic. I thought I was too old to feel that way again. After all these years and...well..." I stopped myself from going into details about my failed marriage and the reasons I probably shouldn't believe in romance at all anymore. "After everything," I settled on the word, "you hit a point where you kind of stop believing it can happen, you know?"

With a huff, Elise put her crochet project in her lap and stared at me. "I'm much closer to having a foot in the ground than you are, young lady."

I tried not to react to the absurd way I'd been addressed.

"If I can still believe in love at my *very* advanced age," Elise continued, "then there is no reason you shouldn't. Especially when it sounds like that's exactly what's happened here."

"It's not that I *do*n't believe in it. I just wasn't sure it could still happen to me." I closed my eyes for a minute, shocked by my own use of the word. "And you? You do still believe in love?"

Elise grew quiet, but after a moment she nodded. "I do."

"Will you tell me about your love story?" Elise could have very easily said no. After all, they'd only just met. But I didn't think she would. For the same reasons that made me want to open up to Elise, I was fairly sure the feeling was mutual.

Sure enough, after a moment, Elise spoke again. "I don't know if you could call it a love story. Doesn't there have to be a happily ever after to qualify?"

"I think that's only for fiction. Real life doesn't always have happy endings."

Elise nodded sadly and focused on her crochet. "I tried not to fall in love," she said slowly. "I did my best to avoid Alex and put my head down and get my job done. I knew that even if Alex returned the feelings that I didn't even understand myself, we could never be together. We came from very different worlds. Maybe I didn't know much about love. But I knew enough to know that those worlds could never cross."

It had all happened so long ago, but it was clear that to Elise, it was just like yesterday. "I'd been working here for just over a year before I got transferred to the front desk." Her eyes flickered momentarily to the counter, where a handful of employees were buzzing around. "After that, it became almost impossible to avoid Alex when they came to the inn. Which felt like it continued to increase in frequency. I know it wasn't real, but it felt like they were always here. Every time I turned around, Alex was there. After a while, it was clear that my feelings were reciprocated." Elise smiled at the memory. "We exchanged little glances for months before, finally, I made a bold move."

"*You* made the move?" I couldn't hide my surprise. It wasn't that I was so old-fashioned, but all those years ago, it would have been almost unheard of for Elise to make any move at all.

"I did." Her eyes sparkled. "It was a rare moment when we were alone, and I couldn't stop myself. I knew I could be fired for what I did. After all, Alex's family were always such important guests. Or even worse, I could have been rejected. But it didn't matter. My heart was so full of what I felt for Alex that I just had to do it."

I clasped my hands together. "And…"

"It was the most magical kiss I've ever experienced. Except, of course, for all those that came afterward." She winked, and I couldn't help but laugh.

"It sounds to me like a very happy ending, if you ask me."

"Oh, my dear. That was simply the beginning. And just like with fiction, the beginning of a story is always full of hope."

I sat back in the chair as if all the air had been sucked out of my lungs. It was true. The beginnings of these kinds of stories were always so hopeful and then…

"Would you be a dear and fetch me a chamomile tea?" Elise's question brought me back to the moment. "I'm afraid I'll never be able to sleep after all that sugar."

I tucked the precious letter that was still on my lap back into my purse and nodded, grateful for the distraction to collect my thoughts. "Of course. I'll be right back."

It was almost dark outside now, but the lobby of the inn still managed to feel warm and welcoming with the light from the fire and all the candles and lanterns that had been set out. I made my way to the drink cart and set out two cups with chamomile tea bags. Right as I was pouring the boiling water, the room was once more filled with light.

A small cheer went up from the staff and a few of the guests groaned, making me grin. I had to admit, the candle-light had been nice and provided a nice backdrop to the story I was telling Elise. But maybe if the lights had come back on, there was a chance that the roads would open.

Holding on to that little bit of hope, I took the two cups of tea and made my way to the front desk.

"Sorry to bother you. I'm sure you have your hands full with—"

"Mrs. McCormick." Lucy's head shot up and if she was frazzled in any way, it didn't show on her kind face. "You're no bother at all. What can I help you with?"

"The power's back," I stated the obvious. "And I was hoping that meant that maybe…"

"It's just the backup generators." Lucy pressed her lips together. "It took longer than expected to get them up and running, but unfortunately we don't expect the power back on for another few hours, maybe even a few days depending on how bad the storm is."

"A few days?"

"Not to worry," Lucy said quickly. "The backup generators will be enough to handle our needs here."

I didn't seem to realize that it wasn't the power that I cared all that much about. Then again, how could she? "What about the roads? Are they open yet?"

"Not that I've heard." The innkeeper shook her head. "Which is probably a good thing."

I was startled. "How could that be a good thing?"

"We had to adjust our bookings because of the storm," the woman patiently explained. "It doesn't happen often, but when it does, we often have to extend some reservations for guests who can't leave. It usually all balances out with the guests who can't make it through the storm. With such a small inn, and only sixteen rooms, it can be a bit of a shuffle sometimes."

"Wow. I guess I never thought of that." I moved to leave. "You're all so busy. I'll let you get back to work."

"Like I said, it's no problem at all," Lucy said gently. "Is there a particular guest I can check on for you?"

The woman's question took me off guard, and my face heated with a blush. I hadn't mentioned that I was meeting anyone at the inn when I'd arrived. Mostly because it felt a little bit illicit and I'd never done anything so reckless before that I wasn't entirely sure how to handle the situation on any level. Although I was quickly growing weary of worrying about anyone else's opinions on the situation.

"Was it that obvious?"

Lucy chuckled a little. "It really is none of my business who you are waiting for, or why. But if I can help you in any way, I'd be happy to."

I'd hesitated to ask after Adam because there was a part of me that was afraid of the answer. I already knew he wasn't coming. But what I didn't know was whether it was because of the storm or because of some other reason. *What if he got cold feet? What if, after all these years, he'd never intended to meet me? What if he'd decided to stand me up? Again.*

I'd have my answer with one simple question. But what if I didn't like that answer?

I glanced behind me at Elise, who'd picked up her crocheting again. Talking to the older woman had been a nice surprise, and for the first time in a long time, I'd been able to talk about him with an impartial person. It felt good.

"No." I made my decision. Some things were better not to know. Or at least, to postpone the knowing. "Not right now."

Nine Months Ago...

March

"Don't you think the anticipation is the best part?" Milena, Cal's fiancée, who I always thought was the most romantic of all of my daughters-in-law, leaned forward on the table and put her chin in her hands.

"The best part?" Jade lifted her head from the baby at her breast. "It would be torture."

"I think torture is a little extreme." Gwen, her eldest son's fiancée, joined them at the table with a tray of cookies. "But I definitely don't think the anticipation would be the best part." She shot Milena a look. "I can't believe you haven't even heard his voice yet."

All eyes were once again on me. I wasn't sure how the conversation had focused on me in the first place, and I wasn't entirely comfortable discussing my...*situation* with my son's fiancées and wives. Not that the women had any compunction about talking about it with me. From the moment I'd stepped foot into Jade's kitchen, I'd been the topic of discussion.

"I don't think that—"

"Isn't it kind of suspicious that he doesn't want to talk on the phone?" Jade interrupted. "I know Mitch is concerned about—"

"Mitch doesn't need to be concerned about anything." I stopped my daughter-in-law. "I'm an adult, and I can take care of myself. Besides, don't the two of you have your hands full right now?"

I used my head to gesture to the newborn Jade was currently feeding.

My first grandchild, Clara McCormick, had been born only a month earlier, at the end of February. After some initial worry during pregnancy that there might be complications with the baby, she was born totally healthy and absolutely perfect. I was completely smitten with her and tried to spend as much time as I possibly could helping out at Mitch and Jade's house while also respecting their space. I was finding it to be a delicate balance, which is why I was thrilled when Mitch arranged for all the ladies to come over for the afternoon.

I'd even put up with the younger women's nosy questions if it meant I could sneak in some extra granddaughter cuddle time.

"We definitely do have our hands full," Jade admitted. She readjusted the baby at her breast and sank back against the couch cushion. "I swear, all I do is sit right here and make milk. I feel like a—"

"Don't say it." Evie stopped her. "This phase will pass." She offered Jade a reassuring smile. "They're always like this at first. All they do for the first month or two is sleep and eat."

"And poop." Milena giggled.

"Does she ever poop." Jade laughed. "Fortunately, Mitch handles a lot of the diapers."

"I never thought I'd see the day." I shook my head. "He really is a good father."

Jade's face lit up. "I'm so lucky."

"It has nothing to do with luck." Gwen sat on the couch next to Jade. "Amazing attracts amazing." She squeezed Jade's arm lightly. "Besides, you've trained him well."

The ladies laughed and for a moment, I forgot they'd been interrogating me about Adam and the letter I'd received on New Year's Eve.

Unfortunately, Gwen hadn't. "You do have to admit that it's a little unusual." She shifted the topic of conversation easily back to me. "Writing letters is very…"

"Romantic," Evie filled in.

"I was going to say archaic."

My mouth dropped open.

"I think it's very romantic, Maureen."

"Thank you, Evie."

"What's romantic?" Amber appeared in the doorway, holding a tray with a tinfoil-wrapped plate.

"Maureen's letters."

"Ohh." Amber set the plate on the table and took a seat across from me. "I agree. *So* romantic."

"But you have to admit," Jade said. "It is unusual."

"Of course it's unusual," Evie said in support. "But the whole situation is unusual. When was the last time you heard of two lovers reconnecting after almost forty years."

"I don't know if lover is…"

"You *were* lovers, weren't you?" Amber stared at me, eagerly waiting for an answer.

The last thing I wanted to talk about with the girls was my sex life. Even if it had taken place so long ago. Yet, I also knew when I was outnumbered. They were not going to be satisfied until they got some details. Not that there were very many to give out. Even if I wanted to. Which I really didn't.

Amber wiggled her eyebrows, and I couldn't help but laugh at the girl I'd come to love as my own daughter despite the fact that she and her sister Chelsea were both constant reminders of my husband's long-running affair. There had been a time not too long ago when I wouldn't have been able to be in the same room as either of the girls, but that was also when I couldn't bear to return to Cedar Springs either. So much had changed.

My sons had believed for years that the reason we'd left the lake house after learning of Harold's affair and secret family was because the memory of learning about my husband's betrayal in my favorite place was too much for me to bear. But it couldn't have been further from the truth.

It was true that I had known of Harold's affair for years. Just as I'd known about Chelsea and Amber's existence. I'd never told anyone about what I knew because I'd secretly hoped I would never have to. Naively, I'd assumed that if I ignored the fact that my husband had a secret life, we could all go on existing as we always had. I'd keep looking the other way, Harold could have it all, and my boys would never need to know about their father's betrayal.

Of course, things hadn't turned out the way I'd hoped. Not even close.

I remembered the day that everything had changed as clearly as if it were yesterday. It was the night of the summer solstice festival and dance. It was also my favorite night of summer, but not for the reasons everyone else had.

As the boys had gotten older, I'd gradually bowed out of attending the festivities in favor of spending the night alone. I'd sit on the deck, sipping a glass of wine and allow myself the luxury of remembering.

It was the one night a year when I would allow myself to think of the life I could have had. With Adam. Deep down, I knew it wasn't fair to my husband or my family to hold any kind of feelings for another man—or another life—at all. But I'd convinced myself that one night a year couldn't hurt.

Until that night.

The boys had gone to the dance. Their father was late coming from the city, and I had just assumed he'd go straight to the festival the way he always did. If Harold knew why I preferred not to attend the summer solstice festival when I enjoyed all the others so much, he never said. But that night, instead of going straight to town, he'd come by the house. To talk.

It was over. He could no longer lead two lives, and he'd made the decision to leave me and the boys to be with his other family.

Just like that, my world imploded, and I knew at once that I was at fault.

I'd never loved Harold the way he'd deserved. Logically or not, I blamed Cedar Springs, the lake, the summer solstice festival, and the memories that I just couldn't seem to let go for the destruction of my family.

Somehow, Ian had sensed that something was amiss and had returned early after dropping his brothers off at the dance to find me quietly crying on the deck. My eldest son, the same age as I'd been when I'd fallen so deeply in love with Adam in that very spot, sat with me while I sobbed.

The next day, we'd packed up and returned to the city. Maybe it was to punish myself or maybe it was to protect my heart, but I could never bring myself to return until recently, when Declan convinced me I couldn't miss Mitch and Jade's surprise wedding.

Maybe it was the love my sons had all found in the same place that held that magic for me, maybe it was just the passing of time, or maybe I just finally understood that my memories from so long ago weren't to blame for my husband's infidelities. Whatever it was, I was long past punishing myself.

"You know what I think?" I put both hands flat on the table and looked around the room. I waited a beat before zeroing in on Jade, who'd shifted the baby to her shoulder to burp. "I think I've waited long enough for baby snuggles."

A few of the women protested, but Jade dutifully handed over the baby. I spent a few minutes cooing over the little girl and dropping kisses on her tiny cheeks.

"I appreciate everyone's interest in my life," I said when I looked up again.

"Your *love* life." Gwen giggled but I simply shook my head and ignored her.

"Adam is an old friend, and I'm very much enjoying reconnecting with him again. I assure you all that there is nothing suspicious or odd about writing letters back and forth. Not everyone was born in a technical age. Letters are a perfectly normal way to communicate."

"I think it's *so* romantic." Milena sighed. "Do you think Cal would write me letters?"

"I think Cal would do whatever you asked him to," Evie said with a laugh. "That boy is totally smitten with you."

Milena blushed, but it was true. All my sons were completely taken with their women. It made me feel better about my own decisions that I'd somehow still managed to raise good boys, who'd turned into better men who loved their women fiercely.

"Maureen, will you tell us about him?" I turned to see Amber watching me carefully. "I mean, I know you might not want to tell the guys all the dirty details, and I'm not suggesting you tell them to us either," she added quickly. "Unless you want to." Again, she wiggled her eyebrows. "But maybe a few details?"

"Like how you met?" Evie asked.

"Or your first date?" Milena leaned forward. "I bet he picked you up at your front door with flowers."

It didn't matter how much time had passed, I remembered

those days as if they'd been yesterday. "We met at the summer solstice dance," I told the girls.

"I'm sorry I'm late!" Chelsea burst into the room in a whirlwind of color and noise. She and her boyfriend Lucas were always on the move, traveling from place to place, and although the nomadic life seemed to suit her, it had also made her perpetually late to…well, everything. She bent to kiss me on the cheek and fussed over baby Clara, who'd fallen asleep in my arms. "Are we talking about the dance?" she asked as she moved away to find a seat. "I love the summer solstice dance."

"We're talking about the dance *forty* years ago," Gwen said. "Maureen was about to tell us how she met Adam."

"*The* Adam?" Chelsea's mouth dropped open. "You met him at the dance? They had that way back then?"

I pressed my lips together and shot an unimpressed look at the youngest of the women. "First of all, it wasn't quite forty years ago. And, yes. They certainly did. And just like it is now, the festival was the kick-off to summer."

"And love." Amber drew out the word and burst into giggles.

"Do you want to hear about how we met or not?"

"And your first date," Milena added, lest she forget.

Resigned that I was not going to get away without giving them some details, I took a sip of my tea and for the first time in a very long time started to tell the story.

Thirty-Seven Years Ago

The cool lake water soothed my aching feet. I let out a satisfactory sigh and laid back on the dock next to Sue Ann.

"I told you not to wear those shoes."

I didn't bother opening my eyes. I knew without looking that Sue Ann would have her *I told you so* look on her face.

"The shoes were perfect with that dress and you know it." I stretched my arms up over my head and sighed again. "Besides, the blisters are totally worth it. I wouldn't change a thing."

After that first dance together, Adam had simply moved straight into the second song by mutual agreement, and then the third. We'd danced our way all around the floor, completely unaware of anyone else.

"It was like something out of a movie."

Next to me, Sue Ann giggled. The dock beneath us moved as she flipped to her side. I fin*ally* opened one eye to see her staring at me. "Tell me everything," Sue Ann said. "I want all the details."

I didn't have to be asked twice. I'd been dying to talk about the boy—the *man*—who'd swept me off my feet. Literally.

"Isn't he handsome?" I flipped over to my side. "Those eyes." I sighed and squeezed my own eyes shut, remembering the way he'd looked at me as if I were the only girl at the dance.

"He *is* handsome," Sue Ann agreed. "But a little old for you, don't you think? I mean...you *just* turned eighteen, Maureen. He has to be at least thirty."

My eyes snapped open, and I stared at the girl who was supposed to be my very best friend. "I turned eighteen over four months ago, Sue Ann. I'm practically an adult."

"Practically," her friend murmured under her breath.

"And he is *not* thirty." Truthfully, I didn't know how old Adam was. It was obvious that he was older than me. Especially considering he'd told me he'd just finished university. But he couldn't be more than four or five years older, and that was a perfectly acceptable age gap. I told my friend as much.

"Besides, I'm very mature for my age. A few years doesn't make any difference at all."

Sue Ann didn't look convinced. She raised an eyebrow and made an annoying clicking sound with her tongue. "You do know what boys that age want from younger girls, don't you?"

My stomach clenched, but not in a painful way, and a shot of excitement flew through my body. "Do you really think so?"

"Maureen!"

Sue Ann was thoroughly scandalized, but I could only laugh.

"I guess we'll find out," I commented off-handedly, causing Sue Ann to squeal again. "He asked me if he could take me for ice cream."

"What?" Sue Ann sat up straight on the dock and grabbed my hands. "How could you not tell me that? You're going on a date? Tonight?"

"Ice cream." I tried *but* failed to sound casual about it. Especially because I felt anything but casual about it. "He's picking me up at seven."

"What are we doing out here?" Sue Ann jumped to her feet. "We have to pick out your outfit."

I laughed and let my friend drag me up the dock toward the house.

A few hours later, dressed in stonewash denim shorts and a black tank top with a matching denim jacket that Sue Ann assured me looked very mature, I was ready for my date when Adam picked me up in his uncle's borrowed car. He rang the doorbell like a gentleman and shook my father's hand politely.

I was certain I heard my sister giggle when Adam handed me the bouquet of daisies he'd no doubt picked alongside the road where they were currently growing in abundance, and tied with twine. They were the most beautiful flowers I'd ever seen, and I knew without looking that my older sister would be simply green with envy at the handsome young man picking me up for a date and bringing me flowers.

Not that I bothered to spare Linda a glance. I was far too smitten with Adam, who, as soon as it was polite to do so, excused us so we could go to town for ice cream.

I'd been so worried that the magic from the night before at the dance wouldn't shine so bright the next day, but I shouldn't have wasted my time with such thoughts because the moment he opened the door for me and his hand gently brushed my arm as I sat in the front seat, the sparks flew once more.

"You look very pretty tonight, Maureen." Adam held my gaze.

"So do you." My blush burned my cheeks. "I mean…you look very handsome."

"Oh." He pretended to look disappointed. "Too bad, because I really was going for pretty."

We both laughed as we drove down the gravel lane, and the nervousness between us vanished. Being with Adam felt easy, like I could be myself. But at the same time, when I was near him, the air felt like it was charged with something. It was both comfortable and exciting at the same time.

"I bet you like chocolate," Adam guessed as we walked toward Sandy's Scoops, the ice cream stand that set up for business on the edge of the beach every season.

"Chocolate?" I stared at him. "Do I look like a girl who likes chocolate?"

"Don't all girls like chocolate?" Adam laughed. "At least, most girls like chocolate. It's a well-known fact."

I pretended to be offended and put my hands on my hips. "Well. There's something you should know about me, Adam."

He paused as we reached the end of the road that led to the beach. "And what's that?"

I stopped and looked him in the eye, with a sassy smile. "I am not *most* girls." I winked before hopping down from the asphalt and onto the sandy beach.

Behind me, I heard him chuckle. "No, Maureen. You most certainly are not most girls."

I ended up ordering a strawberry waffle cone and Adam got a scoop of chocolate. Like most summer nights, the beach was still full of people. Some still swimming, because the sun didn't set until past nine so early in the summer, but most camped out on blankets, enjoying the late evening heat before packing up for the day.

Naturally, we started to walk away from the crowds, farther down the beach, where the sand got rougher and old logs from the mill on the other side of the lake had washed up over the years.

I climbed up on a big log and swung my feet while Adam leaned on one hip next to me.

"So is it just ice cream? Or do you not like chocolate at all?"

I laughed, amused at his interest in my dislike of something so popular. "I love hot chocolate," I said. "But when it comes to ice cream, there are just better options, you know?"

"And you always go for the better option?"

I dropped my chin and looked up at him through my eyelashes. "I'm here with you, aren't I?"

I should have been shocked by my boldness, but just like everything else with Adam, it felt natural.

"I don't know if I'm the *better* option," he said with a shake of his head. "But I sure am glad that you're here with me. I had a lot of fun last night."

"You're a very good dancer."

"I had an excellent partner."

We flirted back and forth until our ice cream was gone and the sun started to sink behind the mountain.

"I should probably take you home."

I sighed deeply, knowing it was the right thing to do, although it was the last thing I wanted. I might be eighteen, but I was still under my father's roof and there were expectations. I was a *good girl*, after all.

"Okay." I hopped off the log. "But only on one condition."

Adam tilted his head and humored me. "And what's that?" He took a step closer to me.

"Will you agree to take me out again?"

"Absolutely. On one condition."

"You can't make a condition on a—oh." The words fell from my lips as Adam took another step and reached out with a hand to cup my cheek. My stomach flipped, and I hardly dared to breathe. *Was he going to kiss me? On our first date?*

I'd only been kissed once before. But it didn't count when my next-door neighbor, whom I'd grown up with, kissed me smack on the lips in the playground in seventh grade at lunchtime. I had given him a sharp knee to the groin and he'd dropped like a sack of flour. We'd both ended up in the principal's office—which, to this day, I thought was a massive injustice.

And there was the kiss in Sue Ann's basement with Conrad, a friend from school when we were playing spin the bottle. But I didn't count that either. It was messy and wet and the only thing that made me feel was disgust.

But I wasn't thinking of the neighbor boy or the sloppy kiss in Sue Ann's basement at that moment. Not with Adam standing so close I could feel his breath on my lips, the slightest trace of chocolate in the air, his palm heating my skin. Ever so slowly, as if I were a fawn that would be scared away if he moved too quickly, he stroked my cheek until I closed my eyes, a small sigh slipping from my lips.

And then his lips were on mine. So soft, I could hardly feel them at first. A flutter. Barely a touch. And then more as his mouth pressed onto mine. I'd been afraid that I wouldn't know what to do, but I needn't have worried. My mouth moved, just a little, in response to him. It wasn't too much. But it was perfect and just enough to send my heart soaring.

When the kiss was over, all too quickly, he pulled away, and my eyes fluttered open. Adam's lips were curled up in a sweet smile, as if kissing me had been the sweetest surprise. It certainly had been for me. I was already anticipating the next one.

He took my hand with a shy smile and together we walked down the beach toward Main Street.

I didn't know exactly how yet, but I knew this summer was going to change my life. Forever.

Chapter Four

Present

"YOU TOLD your girls that story, too?" Elise took a sip of the chamomile tea I had brought her. "That's very brave of you."

I laughed. "Some might say it wasn't a great decision. But I think it was time to tell them something about Adam after so much time had passed."

Elise nodded. "Probably true." She held her mug with shaking hands and inhaled deeply. "There's just something so soothing about chamomile tea, don't you think?"

I nodded and settled into the chair across from her. I'd barely taken my first sip when Elise picked up the thread of our conversation.

"He was your first love."

It wasn't a question, but I nodded without hesitation. "I fell hard and fast after that."

"All it took was one kiss?"

I laughed. I'd like to say that it took more than that, but it hadn't. Not really. Certainly, there was a lot more to our relationship than the sweet kisses that, over time, became a lot more urgent and insistent. But I'd known then, just as I still knew now, that it had been that first perfect kiss that had sealed my fate.

"I know it sounds silly," I told Elise. "Especially now that I'm older and wiser about these things." I chuckled a little to myself. "Or at least I'd like to think I am. The moment I saw him at the dance, I knew there was something special about him. But when we kissed, it was as if everything became crystal clear, and I just knew."

"Knew he was the one?"

I hesitated but finally nodded. "Just like that. I knew I loved him." I looked up at Elise. "Do you think that's silly or naive?"

"Not at all." Elise's voice was soft, her eyes glassy. "I felt the same way after that very first kiss with Alex."

I sipped at my tea. "You mentioned that the beginning of your story was full of hope." I knew I was taking a chance asking Elise more questions, and I didn't want to be too pushy or forward, but at the same time, it felt like we were past that part of our new friendship. And something told me that Elise wanted to talk just as much as I did.

"It *was* full of hope," she said after a moment. "Just like you described it to be with Adam. That's how I felt with Alex. Like we could take on the world. As long as we were together, everything would be fine."

Something in her tone told me that it wasn't fine at all. "And then?"

"And then reality intruded." Elise curled her lips together so they almost disappeared. She lifted her tea to her mouth and blew carefully over the hot surface before taking a tentative sip. It was only then that she spoke again. "Alex's father was never going to accept our relationship. Even if he did like me and think of me as a quality employee at his favorite inn. That's all I'd ever be, working class. While Alex was the heir to the family business and that came with *expectations*."

"Did Alex tell him about the two of you?"

Elise shook her head. "It was never an option. We knew that. The world was…well, it was different back then. Even after I was promoted to front desk manager, which was simply unheard of for a woman back then, that was as much as I could ever hope for."

Her eyes took on the now familiar faraway look as she spoke.

"So you just kept sneaking around?" It sounded awful to me to have to hide true love like that for years on end. But maybe having love, even in secret, was better than not having it at all.

"We did. For years, when Alex would visit the inn, we could be together. And as a senior employee, I could find all kinds of reasons that I might need to go down the mountain to town and volunteer to be the one to run any errands that required a trip. But after a while, I had to call an end to it."

"Oh no." I leaned forward. "Why?"

"I loved Alex too much not to." She took another sip of tea and, with a shaking hand, set the cup down on the end table. "Mr. Milsrise was insistent that Alex marry and give him heirs to the family fortune. At that time, their business was thriving. They started spending more and more time up at Merry Falls Inn, entertaining suitable families and candidates for marriage."

"Like an arranged marriage?" I didn't bother hiding my surprise. Even for the time, it seemed extremely old-fashioned.

"Not quite." Elise shrugged. "But not too far off. There were plenty of suitable marriage candidates for Alex. Mr. Milsrise made sure of that."

"And Alex just agreed to it? Just like that?"

"There was no other choice," she said sadly. "Not back then. It didn't take long until the wedding was announced and my heart broke."

My heart broke for my new friend and the pain she must have been in so many years ago.

"For a while, I thought about leaving the inn altogether and finding a new job far away, where I wouldn't have to witness the love of my life marry another, but by then, this was my home. I didn't know anything else. And I think part of me decided that it was better to be near Alex, in at least some small way, than not at all."

"That's heartbreaking."

"It was." Elise smiled sadly. "But it was a long time ago. And I was right. It was better to have pieces of Alex, even if from afar, than nothing at all. Especially when their little girl was born. I can't imagine not having had Susan in my life."

My eyes widened as I put the pieces together. "Your niece?"

Elise winked. "It was Alex's greatest gift to me, allowing me the space to be close to Susan. When she was born, I knew I would never move away."

"That's so sad."

"Is it?" Elise looked me straight in the eye. "Isn't it better to be surrounded by love than to be alone? I had little Susan. She filled my heart in ways I didn't know were possible. It was a kind of love I didn't know existed. If I would have left, I never would have had that."

"But...what about Alex? To just stand by and watch them be a family while you—"

"I was family, too. In a different way." She nodded and clasped her hands together.

For the first time, I noticed the gold band on her left hand. I didn't have a chance to ask before Elise started speaking again.

"After a while, I left the inn and moved down into town to work for a different hotel. Over time, I became the general manager there and held that position until I retired just over twenty years ago. But the Merry Falls Inn was always special to me and held a piece of my heart."

"Which is why you come back every year?"

Elise nodded. "But the most important position I ever held was being Susan's aunt and Alex's best friend. I supported the marriage. How could I not, when little Susan was the product of such a union? So I simply shut off that part of my heart and focused on all the other parts. And there were many. It was a full life I had. With more love than I ever could have imagined."

She finished talking and laid her head back against the chair, as if telling her story had taken all her energy. Maybe it had. Elise's eyes were closed for so long, I thought maybe she'd fallen asleep.

I waited and sipped at my tea, thinking about what Elise had said.

The older woman wasn't wrong. There were plenty of kinds of love. I, too, had experienced them. After Adam... there'd been a time when I was sure I would never love again. But if I had let that feeling take hold and take over, I never would have had my boys. And that love was one that was greater than any other.

"Tell me more." Elise spoke, startling me. "About Adam. And your perfect summer."

"Perfect?"

She opened one eye. "Nothing is perfect. But it sounds like it came close."

"You're right," I said. "Nothing is perfect."

"But?"

"You're right. It was as close to perfect as you can get."

Six Months Earlier

June

Cedar Springs was bustling with activity. It seemed that over the years, the summer solstice festival had only grown larger. I hadn't remembered so many vendor stalls set up along Main Street before. But it was more likely that the passage of time had affected my memory.

I hadn't been to the festival since the boys were little. I'd attended a few times, and then when they were older and needed me less, I'd insisted that it was a good opportunity for *their* father to spend quality time with the children. Over time, it turned into their thing, and I was left alone to sit with my memories.

Now, as I walked slowly down the busy street and took in the sights, I knew I'd been wrong to avoid it for so long. I'd been wrong about a lot of things, but there was no point in dwelling on those things because there was nothing I could do about it now.

"Mrs. McCormick!"

I spun at the sound of my name to see young Jonah running through the crowd toward me. At once, a smile lit up my face, and I bent to catch the boy in a hug. Evie's son, Declan's soon-to-be stepson, was a very affectionate nine years old. I had fallen for the boy right away. We'd bonded over ice cream and treats the way all good *grandparent* relationships should, and I'd very quickly started to think of Jonah as my own grandson.

"What did I say about calling me Mrs. McCormick?" I gently chastised him and ruffled his hair.

He shrugged sheepishly. "But then I don't know what to call you. Mom says I can't use your first name because it's not 'spectful."

"Respectful?" I tried not to laugh.

"Yeah. That."

"What about Momo?"

"Momo." Jonah tried out the name. "Momo…yeah. I like that."

"So do I." I stood and offered the boy my hand. "What are you doing, running around? Is your mother here somewhere?"

"She's got a table set up." He pointed down the street toward Evie's store, Live, Love, Lake. "Come on. I'll show you."

With little option, I let myself be led through the crowds toward the booth Evie had set up outside her storefront. Just like the shop itself, the little booth was full of beautiful things. There were a variety of cups and mugs with cute sayings on them. Yummy scented candles and bath products and a selection of locally made jewelry. Evie truly had an eye for gorgeous things, and I wasn't the only one who thought so. Evie's store had been very successful with both tourists and locals, and judging by the lineup of customers waiting to talk to her now and ask her questions, it looked like the summer solstice would be another busy day for her.

"Hi, Mom." Declan emerged from the shop and placed a box under the table before straightening up and looking at me again. "Mom? What are you…you never come to the festival."

I opened my arms for a hug as Declan moved around the table to join me and Jonah. "I thought it was about time," I said when he released me from the embrace. "Long past time, actually."

Declan nodded. "I agree." There was a small, knowing smile on his handsome face.

Out of all my children, Declan was the most in tune with my feelings. Truthfully, Declan was more in tune with *everyone's* feelings. He had a huge heart, which was exactly why he'd spent his life helping others with his charity organization.

There'd been a time when I worried that Declan spent so much time immersed in other people's lives and problems so he wouldn't have to think about his own life. I'd been so concerned that my kind-hearted son would spend his life alone.

I needn't have worried because Evie, who was just as warm-hearted as Declan, and her beautiful son had created the perfect family for Declan.

"Why didn't you come to the festival before, Momo? It's awesome."

"Momo?" Amused, Declan looked between me and Jonah with a raised eyebrow.

"Yes, Momo."

"I like it."

"So do I." I grinned and turned my attention to Jonah. "I agree, Jonah. The festival *is* awesome. I never should have stayed away as long as I did."

"Why did you?"

"Yeah, Mom." Declan *did*n't bother to hide his grin. "Why did you stay away for so long?"

I knew I wasn't going to get away without fessing up, even a little bit. I shot my son a look but bent down to look into Jonah's eyes. "Have you ever had a place that reminds you of someone or some time in your life? Like maybe the playground reminds you of a certain friend?"

The boy nodded. "I think I know what you mean. Like every time I play Mario Kart, I think of my dad because we play it a lot whenever we're together."

"Yes." I smiled warmly. "It's kind of like that. And Mario Kart is a good memory, but sometimes places or things, well… they make you think of sad memories. Or the memory is so good that it makes you kind of sad to be reminded of it."

Jonah screwed up his face. "What's so good it's sad?"

"I know it's hard to understand." I straightened up and looked at Declan, who was watching me with understanding.

"I had no idea, Mom."

"There was no way you could."

There was still so much my family didn't know about Adam and how different my life could have been. They might not ever know, and that would be okay, too. Some memories were best to keep to myself.

"But I'm happy to be here now," I said brightly. "Jonah, what's your favorite part of the summer solstice festival?"

The boy immediately started to chatter about cotton candy, ice cream, and mini donuts.

"Your mother would not be happy if I let you eat all that junk," Declan said. "But maybe we can have one thing," he added with a conspirator's whisper and a wink. "Can you go grab that other box by the counter inside first?"

Jonah didn't have to be asked twice. He took off at a sprint, eager to help...but even more eager for the promised treat.

"He's a good boy." I laughed as he ran off.

"He is." Declan turned his attention back to me. "I really do think it's great that you're here today, Mom. I had no idea that the solstice festival brought up bad memories for you. I just always thought it was a father-son thing."

"They weren't bad memories, Dec." I let my gaze drift down the busy street to where the tents for the band and the dance that would happen later that night were set up. "Those memories were far from bad."

"Maybe it's time for some new memories."

"It absolutely is." I spent another second looking toward the tent before I looked again at Declan and grinned.

"I like seeing you so happy, Mom. It wouldn't have anything to do with a certain pen pal you have, would it?"

I laughed. "You don't think it's silly and old-fashioned that we're only writing letters and haven't met in person yet?"

"Not at all." Declan didn't hesitate. "Like Evie says, the letters are romantic." He shot a glance over his shoulder to where his fiancée was busy with a customer. "Maybe I should write some letters of my own?" He shook his head and focused on me once more. "Besides, you've met before."

"We have."

"And I'm sure you will again. When the time is right."

The idea warmed me through.

"But I trust that when you do meet up, if he asks you to go with him to Africa again, your answer will still be no, right?"

Momentarily confused, I took a step back. I nodded vaguely, recalling the version of the story I'd told Declan that wasn't entirely the truth. Time and distance had a way of changing your memories, and my children never needed to know the way things had really played out.

I remembered. I remembered exactly how the rest of that summer *really* went.

Thirty-Seven Years Ago

"Isn't it amazing, Maureen? I didn't think it was even a possibility, but now..." Adam's eyes took on a faraway look while my own head spun with the information he'd just given me.

Less than an hour earlier, I'd been in my room in my father's lake house, taking care to curl my hair and apply just the slightest amount of Linda's lip gloss that I'd snuck out of her purse. My heart raced with the idea of seeing Adam Lancaster, just the way it had all summer every time he picked me up for a date or—more recently—when we snuck away to the dock hidden in the trees.

We'd exchanged dozens of kisses since that magical first one. As far as I was concerned, there would never be enough kisses to make me happy.

Every time his lips pressed to mine, it was as if I flung out of control. My body went numb, but at the same time felt as if it were on fire. The world spun around us as if we were the only two people in the world.

We'd even had a few times in the back seat of Adam's uncle's car, where he'd been brave enough to slip his hands under my blouse. The first time it happened, I dared not breathe, but it felt so good to have his hands on my body. Together, we'd grown bolder and explored more and more of each other.

When I confessed the details to Sue Ann, my friend never failed to tell me to slow down and be careful. After all, Adam was an older boy, who only wanted one thing from me. But I knew that wasn't true. We didn't spend all our time making out. Mostly, we talked and talked. In only a few short weeks, Adam knew everything about me. My hopes and dreams, even the silly ones. And I, in turn, knew about Adam. There wasn't a doubt in my mind that we were meant to be together. Forever.

There had never been a love like ours. It was so perfect.

Soon, every moment we had was spent together. We'd spend our days at the beach with the other summer kids, playing volleyball or swimming and splashing in the lake. When we wanted to be alone, we'd go for a picnic or hike to one of the natural hot pools higher in the mountains.

Our evenings were spent at bonfires, or walking hand in hand down the beach. Adam had taken me for dinner a few times at the local restaurants, but my favorite nights were spent on the dock on the edge of town that was partly hidden by the trees and far enough away from the lights that when we laid down on the blanket and looked up, the stars were dazzling overhead. I'd lay in his arms, my head on his chest, and count the shooting stars, making wishes on all of them in between kisses until I was dizzy from our love.

Now, with the news he'd just given me, I was dizzy for a totally different reason.

Just as I had every time I met Adam, I ran down to the dock, anticipating yet another kiss.

Instead, when I'd arrived, Adam was pacing on the long, wooden dock. When he saw me, his face lit up. He grabbed my hands and started talking so fast, I could hardly keep up.

"Wait." I shook my head after a few moments and forced myself to look away because I knew without a doubt that I'd agree to anything as long as those sparkling eyes were fixed on me. "You're going where?"

"Africa. Isn't it incredible?"

"Africa?"

"Yes!" He vibrated with excitement. "Well, no."

"No?"

"Maybe." He shook his head, and I worked to keep up. "Nothing is for sure yet, but I've made it to the next round of applicants."

I only had a vague idea of Africa from the little bit I'd learned in school. From what I knew, it was a wild land full of wild animals and wild people, not at all like the safe, suburban world I knew and understood. The concept of Africa at all was so foreign, I couldn't really wrap my mind around it.

"There's such a demand for quality health care there." Adam's voice deepened. He paced to the far end of the dock and shook his head. "It's awful, Maureen. There are so many people, and in so many of the villages, they don't even have the basics, like fresh running water. Can you imagine?"

I couldn't.

"And there's almost no such thing as health care at all. Can you believe it? There are millions of people who don't have any access to the things that we take for granted."

Guilt flared low in my gut. Before meeting Adam earlier in

the summer at the solstice dance, my biggest worries had been about frivolous things: a new dress for the dance, the grades on my final exams, and what college courses to sign up for in the fall.

I'd never once thought about having access to running water, or having a roof over my head. I'd certainly never considered the idea of not having access to health care if I needed it.

Adam made me think of serious things. Real things. He was older than me by seven years, but he was also the smartest, kindest man I'd ever met, and he wanted to make a difference in the world. Even if at eighteen I could hardly understand it, I was very quickly falling in love with his ideals. And him.

"I can't imagine," I admitted after a moment. "It's like a whole other world."

"Exactly." Adam moved so quickly toward me, the dock swayed under our feet. "It *is* a whole other world. Think of the difference I could make there."

I nodded numbly as I tried to process what he was telling me. There was no doubt he could make a huge difference to the people of Africa. *If* he could get accepted into the program. I had no doubt that he would. Adam was perfect for such a thing. *But where did that leave me?*

I forced myself to swallow back my selfishness. "I didn't know you were considering something like that."

For the first time since I'd arrived on the dock, the smile slipped from his boyish face. "I didn't want to say anything at first," he said. "It was a long shot, and we'd only just met. I guess I was hoping…well, I don't know what I was hoping. But I didn't really think anything would come of the opportunity."

"But it has."

He nodded solemnly. "It *maybe* has."

I turned away and walked to the edge of the dock. I stared into the cold, blue lake.

Were there blue lakes like this in Africa?

The thought sprang into my mind so unexpectedly, I started to giggle.

My giggles very quickly turned into full-blown laughter and then, to my horror, sobs.

"Don't cry, Maureen." Adam slipped an arm around my shoulders and pulled me into his chest. "Please don't cry. Nothing is for sure yet. There's still a lot of hoops to jump through, and I haven't made any decisions yet."

But I knew he had.

"And I know it doesn't seem like it right now," he continued. "But this is a good thing. And I know it's unexpected. I mean, already this summer has been unexpected. *You* were very unexpected."

His words stilled me. I swallowed my sobs and wiped at my face, embarrassed I'd let him see me that way. I took a deep breath and turned to face him.

"*You* were very unexpected, too."

Adam put his hands on each of my arms and stared deeply into my eyes. "I won't know anything for a while yet," he said. "Let's not think about it. Not until there's something to think about, okay?"

I nodded in agreement.

"Let's just enjoy our summer. Together."

I nodded again. "I'd like that very much."

I knew I couldn't ignore reality forever. But I was still naive enough to believe that if I didn't think about something, it would just go away.

Adam's lips curled up into a small smile. He used his thumb to stroke my cheek and gently pull me toward him, where he pressed his lips to mine and just like that, I wasn't thinking about anything else but the feel of Adam's lips on mine and how perfect they were.

Chapter Five

Present

"EXCUSE ME, LADIES."

I sat back and wiped at my eye and the tear that I hadn't realized had slipped out as I recounted that summer evening so long ago. My story had been interrupted by a young bellboy, who nodded apologetically in my direction, but focused on Elise. "I thought maybe you ladies would like some cookies, Ms. Bell. They're your favorite."

"Oatmeal chocolate chip?" Elise tilted her head and narrowed her eyes at the plate in front of her.

"Of course, Ms. Bell." The young man held the plate closer.

"You're new here." She took a cookie from the plate. "Have we met?"

He nodded eagerly. "Once before. My name is Max. I've only been here since September."

"Then you know not to call me Ms. Bell." She spoke sternly, but the sparkle in her eye gave her away. "Please," she said, her voice softening. "Call me Elise like everyone else."

"Of course. Elise."

He was rewarded with the older woman's bright smile.

Max offered me a cookie as well. "I was told to check if you'd like dinner in the dining room tonight or here in the lobby with your new friend."

"Dinner?"

I hadn't given any thought to food at all, besides the cookie now in my hand. I'd lost all track of time talking to Elise. Sure enough, when I glanced at the time, it was dinner time. I looked to Elise, who shook her head.

"Not for me," Elise said. "I'm quite comfortable here and not at all hungry. Unless you would like something, Maureen?"

I shook my head. "I think this cookie will hit the spot."

Max looked between us and nodded. "If you change your mind, just let me know. I'd be happy to get you whatever you need."

The poor boy looked a little disappointed that he wasn't able to help. Elise must have noticed as well. "Actually, Max. Would you be a dear and fetch us a fresh pot of chamomile tea from the kitchen? And maybe a few muffins, if the cook has any left over from breakfast."

His face lit up with the task. "Of course, Ms…Elise. I'll be right back with that."

After he left, I couldn't help but giggle. "Poor thing was so eager to please. You're like royalty around here."

"Not royalty." Elise waved a hand away. "More like a pain in the ass."

"You said your niece doesn't know you're here right now."

"Well, she knows I'm at the inn since she brought me like she does every year. I like to come up at Christmas to take in the decorations and the festivities. There's nothing quite like Christmas time up here."

"I can appreciate that."

"But I wanted to be alone tonight, and I knew she had

some work to do. She always does." Elise sat up straight, looking pleased with herself. "So I told her I was off to bed early and snuck down here."

"You're quite the rebel." I laughed.

The older woman winked and sat back as Max reappeared with a tray laden with a fresh pot of tea, muffins, and a bowl of grapes. It wasn't until he left under assurances from Elise that she would let him know if there was anything else she needed that Elise picked up the thread of her story again.

"Adam's news must have put quite a damper on the rest of your summer."

"Not at all." I shook my head. I chose a muffin off the tray and picked at the paper wrapper. "In fact, we didn't talk about it at all."

"How could you just ignore such a thing between you?"

I looked seriously at my new friend. "Probably the same way you did with Alex."

Elise sat back in her chair. She was silent for a moment but then she nodded. "Sometimes it's just easier to pretend than to face the truth. At least for a little while. But it never works forever, does it?"

I could sense that Elise wasn't ready to tell me more about Alex. At least not yet.

"No," I admitted. "Hiding from reality didn't work forever. But it definitely worked for a little while." My face warmed with the memories of our summer together. "And I'm sure glad it did."

―――――――

Thirty-Seven Years Ago

It had been weeks since Adam had brought up the awful idea of moving to Africa at the end of summer. I had put it out of my head. Mostly. Only occasionally did I let myself think about what it might mean if the opportunity came to fruition. Would he really leave Cedar Springs, and me, at the end of the summer? Sure, I had planned to leave Cedar Springs at the end of August, too. But that was different. I'd be going to college. This was so very different. Adam was talking about Africa.

Africa!

It was a whole world away.

Ever since that evening on the dock, we'd managed to avoid discussing the future in any specific way. Sure, we spoke about generalities and how one day I dreamed of children and a family of my own. But mostly, we spoke about the present, and we lived for the moment.

And living in the moment was exactly what I planned to do that night.

My mother and father had gone to the city for a few days, and I'd begged and bribed my older sister to sleep at a friend's house. It had cost me a week's worth of chores and my favorite sweater, but it would be worth it to spend time alone with Adam.

We'd planned to spend the evening on the beach at a bonfire with our friends, but when Adam came to the door to pick me up, I held it open. "Why don't you come in for a bit first?"

I batted my eyelashes in a way that felt ridiculous, but judging by the way Adam looked at me, had been just as effective as I'd hoped.

"My parents are gone for the night," I added when he hesitated. "Linda is at a friend's. We have the house to ourselves."

Realization as to what exactly I was saying to him dawned slowly on Adam's handsome features until his mouth hung open slightly. "You mean…you want…I should…"

I nodded and held out my hand.

He took it and allowed me to lead him inside. "I wasn't expecting this." He held me gently in his arms, and I knew in that moment I'd made the right decision. Sue Ann would be scandalized to know I wasn't planning to wait until marriage, but I had never felt anything more right than when I was with Adam. There wasn't a doubt in my mind that we would be together forever.

He lowered his head and kissed me gently. "I love you, Maureen."

The words flowed through me, lighting little explosions of happiness throughout my body. My heart soared. "I love you, too, Adam. So much."

He kissed me again, more urgently this time.

Heat pooled between my legs and something low in my gut clenched. It felt like my body was on fire as he deepened the kisses and our tongues twisted together. I was out of breath, my chest rising and falling quickly, as I pulled away from him. "Come with me."

I led him upstairs to my bedroom and my tiny twin bed.

Adam hesitated in the doorway. "Are you sure?"

"I've never been more sure." I undid the buttons of my blouse and let it fall back off my shoulders, to prove my point.

His nostrils flared a little. He stepped into the room, toward me. "You are gorgeous, Maureen. The most beautiful girl in the world." He kissed me again. This time his hands traveled to my breasts before circling behind my back to unclasp my bra.

I gasped as my breasts were exposed, but then Adam was pulling his own shirt off, and we were skin to skin, our kisses and our need growing in urgency.

"You're sure?"

Wrapped tight in his arms, his hot skin pressed against mine, I had never been clearer of anything else in my entire life. I tilted my head up so I could look into his eyes and whispered, "Yes. I'm so sure."

He kissed me again. "I love you, Maureen. I didn't know it was possible to feel this way about someone else."

My heart soared.

I knew I should be nervous for my first time, but I felt nothing but confident and secure. Adam had that effect on me. He just made everything feel...right.

I pulled from his arms long enough to undo the button on my skirt. The fabric fell to the ground around my feet. I watched as Adam shed his pants and boxers.

I couldn't have hid the little gasp that slipped from my lips if I'd tried. At eighteen, my experience with boys was very limited, and it certainly had never included any nudity. I'd never seen a naked man before and the sight of Adam sent shock waves of excitement through me.

He tilted his head in question. "You're still—"

"I'm very sure." To prove my point, I stepped forward, closing the distance between us, and ran my hands down his bare chest. He shivered from my touch. It made me feel powerful and more in control, despite the fact that everything inside me felt out of control...in the very best possible way.

We kissed and touched and explored each other for what felt like hours. Neither of us were in a rush. Each of us grew bolder with our touching and exploration until finally Adam leaned over the side of the bed and rummaged through the pocket of his discarded pants for the condom, he'd later tell me, he carried around *just in case*.

I was on my back.

Adam held himself up, hovering just over me. He brushed a strand of hair from my cheek. "I'll go slow."

I nodded and bit my bottom lip.

He pressed his lips to mine as he entered me.

A gasp slipped from my lips as my body stretched, and he froze. "No," I said quickly. "It's fine."

And it *was* fine.

In the bathrooms at school, the girls would gossip and giggle about how painful sex would be and how awful and awkward it would be. But as Adam filled me completely, the only thing I could think of was just how wrong they all were because I'd never felt anything quite so perfect in my entire life.

I opened my eyes to see him watching me with a mixture of concern and lust on his handsome face. I smiled and nodded a little. It was all the reassurance he needed. When Adam began to move inside me, the feeling of perfection exploded into one of sheer pleasure.

It wasn't long before my fingers dug into his shoulder, I squeezed my eyes shut tight, and a moan I didn't know I was capable of slipped from somewhere deep inside me. Above me, Adam made a similar noise; his body shuddered, and he collapsed next to me on the bed. He pulled me toward him until my head rested on his chest and held me.

We lay like that, his hands stroking my hair and my back until we both fell asleep, and I couldn't imagine anything ever feeling so perfect.

Four Months Earlier

September

The end of summer had always been bittersweet for me. Years earlier, the shorter days, cooler nights, and the slow changing of the leaves had historically meant that it was time to pack up the boys and start thinking about returning to the city for the start of school. Those last few days before leaving, there had always been an urgency in the air as I tried to pack all the remaining bits of summer fun into a short time. It was exhausting and a little stressful.

But more than that, it had been incredibly sad.

Leaving Cedar Springs in the fall filled me with an intense melancholy, the likes of which I'd only felt once before, also at the end of a summer at the lake. For weeks once I returned to the city with the boys, I would mope around the house, take long naps to pass the days, and find myself staring vacantly into space.

When the boys were still in grade school, Harold insisted that I talk to a psychologist about my depression. I had made the appointment, but I'd canceled it two days before I was supposed to go. I knew what was wrong with me, and it wasn't anything a stranger would be able to help me with.

I couldn't avoid the end of summer, just as I couldn't avoid my memories. I just needed to work through it and move past it. And I always did.

By the end of September, I had once again fallen into the rhythm of daily life in the city. I immersed myself in volunteering at the boys' schools, driving them to their extracurricular activities, and being the best mother I could. Soon, the memories of the summer were just that, memories.

Until the next year.

After the divorce, when I'd stopped my summer visits to Cedar Springs, the fall sadness had disappeared. I was simply too preoccupied with trying to rebuild my life to focus on things I couldn't change. Like the past.

Now, as I walked the quieter streets of Cedar Springs in the first week of September, I was struck by how different the end of summer felt. It was the first autumn since I'd moved there permanently. And, of course, there were the letters from Adam.

Instead of the familiar melancholy, I felt a sense of excitement and hope about the future.

Adam's latest letter was tucked into my purse. I'd read it on the deck that morning while I drank my coffee and then I read it again.

He wanted to arrange a meeting.

The idea thrilled me. But at the same time, it terrified me.

It had been so long since we'd seen each other. An entire lifetime had passed. I was *old*. Then again, Adam was older.

The thought made me giggle as I opened the door to Dream Puffs, the home of the best cinnamon buns in Cedar Springs, or anywhere, as far as everyone in town was concerned. As good as they were, it wasn't the cinnamon buns I preferred.

"What's got you laughing this morning?" Suzy greeted me. "Don't tell me I have flour on my face again." The baker swiped at her face.

"You do," I pointed out. "But that's not why I'm laughing."

"Care to share what's so funny?" Suzy grabbed a napkin and wiped her face before throwing it in the trash. "I could use a laugh today. I got distracted and left a tray of cookies in the oven a few minutes longer than I should have."

"Oh no. I'm sorry to hear that." I did a quick scan at the display case of all the other delicious goodies. "And really, I'm just giggling to myself at an inside joke. It's really nothing to share, sorry."

"It was worth a try. What can I get you today?"

Ever since I was a child, I had loved Dream Puffs's apple Danishes. The recipe had been passed down for generations, and as far as I was concerned, had only gotten better over the years. I had to limit myself to having one only once in a while or on special occasions, or I wouldn't be able to fit into my clothes anymore.

The arrival of Adam's letter was certainly a special occasion.

I ordered myself a warm pastry and a cup of peppermint tea and took both to a quiet table in the corner.

As soon as I was settled, I pulled Adam's letter from my purse.

> *Dearest Maureen,*
>
> *I love hearing about little Clara. Your grand-daughter sounds delightful, and I'm sure she provides you with an endless amount of joy. Sometimes I wonder if I made the right decision by not having a family of my own. It's true, I lived a life of service to others and I've had my share of adventure. But as you know, those experiences came with a certain amount of sacrifice as well.*
>
> *There have been many times, especially in the quiet of the night when I am left with only my own thoughts, that I wonder if I made the right decision.*
>
> *Although, I'm sure most of us feel that way from time to time when it comes to life's bigger choices. No one can really know if the choices they are making are the right ones. And is there ever really a right way to live life?*
>
> *The best we can hope for is to live a life that makes us happy and gives us purpose. I have done that on many levels but as I near the end of my time here, I find that my thoughts turn to other things.*
>
> *It has been such a pleasure getting to know you again, Maureen, through these letters, and I would love nothing more than to see your beautiful smile again.*
>
> *If I may be so bold, I would like to invite you to a very special place I found years ago. Every time I visited*

over the years, I thought of you, and I think you will find it to be a magical place, particularly during the holiday season. I will make all the arrangements and reserve two rooms if you would do me the honor of agreeing to see me again.

Your room will be reserved in your name at Merry Falls Inn in the mountains of North Carolina from December 18-20 to give you plenty of time to return home for little Clara's first Christmas.

I must confess that in anticipation of your agreement, and because the holiday season can be especially hectic, I have already gone ahead and reserved the rooms. Please excuse my boldness. However, in a week's time, I will be heading into the rustic and remote mountains and communication will be difficult for a few months.

I eagerly anticipate returning to civilization and receiving your response. Until then, take care and enjoy your family. Especially that precious little grandbaby.

All my love,
Adam.

I finished re-reading the letter, pushed it to the side and tore off a piece of my Danish.

There was no doubt in my mind about how I would respond. Of course I was going to say yes. The letters we'd exchanged over the last few months had brought some of the brightest spots in my already very bright days. Some of the letters were short, scribbled on the back of an old envelope or recycled paper. Others were pages and pages long, full of details of Adam's life for the last almost forty years.

In return, I had opened up about my marriage to Harold. My summers in Cedar Springs with the boys when they were young. And of course, the divorce, and the quiet years following. I told Adam about all my children, including the girls whom, against all odds, I'd come to love like my own. I detailed their relationships and the new *daughters* and *sons* in my life. I told him how my boys had convinced me to return to Cedar Springs after so many years of staying away. I'd even confessed to him that after the divorce, the reason I'd stayed away from the lake town was to punish myself for the choices I'd made.

I'd wept, while reading and writing the letters, as we both opened up completely.

Even though I hadn't actually heard Adam's voice in decades, I could hear his voice in my head as I read his words, and it was as if no time had passed between us at all.

I'd been given a second chance, and I was old enough to know how rare that truly was.

I put another bite of the warm, pastry in my mouth before pulling my letter writing paper that I'd recently purchased from Live, Love, Lake, along with my favorite pen.

Dear Adam,

I received your latest letter this morning, and immediately I knew that your impending return to North America and civilization deserved a cele-bratory apple Danish from Dream Puffs. I am writing this from a corner table as I enjoy the delicious treat. Do you remember how good they were? I don't know if it's just the passage of time, but they are even sweeter now. One day perhaps you will return to Cedar Springs and experience one for yourself.

As to your question. Of course, my answer is yes. I would be very happy to join you at the Merry Falls Inn. It sounds delightful at Christmas time, and I've never been to North Carolina.

    I hope you have a safe journey and this letter finds you well when you return.

    I very much look forward to seeing you.

    Love always,

    Maureen.

Chapter Six

Present

I WORRIED MAYBE I'd told Elise too much. I'd been caught up in my storytelling. I could hardly believe I'd just told a virtual stranger such intimate details. "I'm so sorry, I never should have—"

"Scandalous." Elise sat back and shook her head. A small, wicked grin slid over her face. "Simply scandalous, Maureen." She wiggled her eyebrows, and I couldn't help but laugh, too.

"It *was.*" I shook my head. "In hindsight, it really was. And I guess by today's standards, it wouldn't even rank on the scandal scale, but at the time…"

Elise nodded. "You loved him."

The laughter on my lips died. "I did," I answered seriously. "Very much." I let my gaze travel toward the front door of the inn again, as if the love I'd felt all those years ago could will him to walk through the door. "Years later, I wondered if it really was love or if I was just too young to understand."

"You understood just fine."

I looked at the older woman. Elise got it. She knew. "I did."

I nodded. "It was true love, and I was absolutely sure that we were meant to be together. Fate had brought Adam Lancaster into my life, and I knew with no uncertainty that he would be my husband."

Obviously, that's not how things played out, but I didn't need to say that out loud.

I put the mostly uneaten muffin back on the plate and sat back with a sigh.

"You haven't mentioned Africa again."

"That's because we never talked about it."

"Not at all?" Surprised, Elise sat up in her chair. "I know you said earlier that you didn't discuss it again, but it just seems like something you would talk about with the love of your life. Did you not speak about the future?"

"Of course we did." I explained to Elise how Adam and I both spoke about the future, without really speaking about the future, almost as if we were planning dream lives with no basis in reality. We discussed how we would split our time between Cedar Springs and exotic cities in Europe like Paris or London. We'd have a nanny to care for all eight of our children while the two of us dined at the best restaurants and shopped for designer clothes. We never once spoke about our careers or what we would do for work or money. It was a lark. A fun game we'd play when I was lying in Adam's arms after we made love.

"It was silly," I told Elise. "But it just seemed easier than talking about the hard stuff. We were young, and I guess I was naive in thinking that if I ignored it, the problem would just go away."

"They never do." Elise shook her head and pressed her lips together. "No matter how much we'd like them to. I played that old game myself long ago."

"Ignoring reality?"

Elise laughed. "Oh yes. Only maybe it was worse because instead of just ignoring reality, I would find myself making up a very pretend world." She sighed deeply. "Our imaginations can be quite powerful."

I sat back and let her continue her own story.

It took Elise a moment, but then she once more started talking. "I told you that Alex's greatest gift to me was allowing me to have a close relationship with Susan."

I nodded.

"Once I moved down into town, I was closer to them a lot more and often got the chance to babysit. But…there were a few occasions when I babysat Susan in their home."

I took a sharp breath, realizing where Elise was going with her story. "You didn't?"

"I did." She nodded once. "When I was alone with the baby in their house, I could pretend that it was my house that I shared with Alex, and little Susan was mine. I never went so far as trying on clothes or jewelry, but when the baby was asleep, I'd walk around the house talking to myself and… well…I did say that our imaginations could be quite powerful."

"You did. But…that must have been so painful."

There was a tear in Elise's eye as she nodded. "But it was as close as I was ever going to get to being married to Alex."

We sat in silence for a few minutes, respecting the pain of unrequited love from so long ago.

"And then one day, Alex came home unexpectedly and caught me talking to myself in the kitchen. After that, I never did it again. Alex never said anything, and thankfully I was still allowed to babysit. But…it never felt the same pretending after that."

"That must have been so hard."

"It was a difficult time." Elise took a deep breath, exhaled slowly, and then once more picked up her crochet project.

"What are you making?"

"A blanket. Susan's daughter is expecting."

"That's so exciting. "I've very recently become a grandmother myself. It's amazing."

"It has been a true blessing to have Susan and then her daughter, Charity. Now…" Elise's eyes shimmered with unshed tears. "So wonderful." She fingered the cream and yellow blanket, examining it for a moment before resuming her stitches. "Although I fear I won't finish."

"When is she due? I'm sure you have time."

Ignoring the question, Elise continued. "The children have been such a blessing in what could have been a very lonely life. Alex was very generous with allowing me to be part of it. I can't imagine life without them all."

"Alex must have loved you very much."

Elise didn't speak for a few minutes, but I didn't miss the tear that slid down her cheek. I was about to apologize for bringing up such a sensitive topic when Elise spoke again.

"Tell me how it happened."

"How what happened?"

"That he went to Africa and you did not."

Thirty-Seven Years Ago

Despite our silly dreams and ridiculous conversations about our futures, both Adam and I knew all too well that none of it was based in reality. And that's what made it so fun and easy.

For a little while.

The reality was that I was scheduled to start school in the fall and Adam…I refused to think about what Adam was going to do, or what would happen if the opportunity in Africa ever came to fruition.

But reality couldn't be ignored forever.

As the summer began to wind down, and we edged ever

closer to the last few weeks of August, it became harder and harder not to think about the one thing we'd avoided talking about. I knew it was only a matter of time before we'd have to face it. The worry of it started to churn in my stomach. The ache in my gut grew worse and worse every day until the day that Adam took my hand and said, "I have news."

I knew with those three simple words that I wasn't going to like what his news was.

Together, we walked to the dock where we'd spent so many private nights. Adam laid out a blanket and pulled a bottle of wine and two glasses from a basket.

I'd only ever had small sips of wine before, at Christmas or on other special occasions. Was *this* a special occasion?

It didn't feel special.

It felt ominous as Adam held out a hand and asked me to come sit with him.

I was stiff as I sat next to Adam on the dock. I pulled my shoes and socks off and stuck my feet in the lake. The cool water snapped me out of my daze. I focused on moving my feet back and forth in the water, watching the bubbles and swirls they left in their wake as Adam removed the cork from the wine and poured us each a small glass.

"What's this for?" I almost hated to ask.

"Just because."

I narrowed my eyes. "Wine is for celebrating."

"Not necessarily." He winked and, before I could protest, leaned over and kissed me slowly.

The feel of his lips on mine dissolved the remainder of the tension I was feeling, and just like that, the worry was gone. Whatever he was going to say, it would be okay. As long as we were together.

"That being said, I do think we should celebrate."

I searched his eyes for a clue, but he gave nothing away.

"I'd like to make a toast." He raised his glass. "To us." He waited until I raised my glass to meet his. "I'm so glad I decided to go to that dance the night I got to town," he said. "And I'm even more glad that I made the decision to buy the really cute girl a glass of lemonade."

I giggled.

"Maureen, you have surprised me from day one."

"Surprised you?" I lowered my glass. "How?"

"I knew you were beautiful." He winked. "That was easy to see. But getting to know you these past few months, I've realized just how smart and funny you are."

"Go on." I wiggled my shoulders and laughed.

"You're kind and caring and…" The smile fell from his face. "You're amazing. I have completely fallen for you, Maureen."

His words were laced with sincerity and despite the fact that we'd told each other dozens of times that we loved each other, there was something special about this time.

With his free hand, he took mine and squeezed. "I love you."

I looked straight into his eyes. "I love you, too, Adam."

We kissed before finally toasting our love.

The wine was sweet, and my tongue tingled with the taste of it. It wasn't until I took my second sip that I remembered. "You said you had news."

I knew before he said anything that it was about Africa. There was only so much denial one person was capable of.

"I heard back from the committee." He kept his gaze fixed on his glass as he spoke. "I've been accepted into the program."

My gut clenched.

"I'll be working with the head optometrist, starting in South Africa. There's a team of us. All kinds of specialists working together to bring health care to so many underprivileged people who might never have the ability to have this kind of care otherwise."

I could tell he was trying to temper his excitement for my benefit.

"That sounds amazing, Adam." It really did sound amazing. "You're going to make such a difference." My heart was breaking, but at the same time, he was so excited I couldn't let him see how devastated I was. My hands shook so badly, I had to put the wine glass down before I spilled all over myself. "The people in Africa are so lucky to have you."

"Come with me."

"What?" I scrunched up my nose. "What did you say?"

"Come with me." Adam reached for my hands and held them tight. "To Africa."

"Africa?" Just saying the word sounded foreign on my tongue, let alone actually *going* there. "I don't...I'm not a doctor."

"There plenty of non-medical roles. It's not just medical personnel. There's a need for facilitators, of course, and people to help with the care of patients and things like water. Can you believe that a huge amount of the population over there doesn't even have access to fresh drinking water? We can make such a difference to so many people, Maureen. Together."

Together. Africa.

My head swam with the possibility. In all my daydreaming, and all our pretending about the future, we never once talked about going to Africa *together*. Was it even possible? Could I go? Did I *want* to go? What would it mean?

Stunned, I looked up at Adam's handsome face. I knew without a doubt that I loved him, but could I leave everything I knew and everything I ever wanted out of life to go with him to the wilds of Africa?

I opened my mouth, but he pressed a finger to my lips.

"Don't answer me right now. It's a huge decision."

I nodded in agreement.

"And I know I just sprung it on you out of the blue. That probably wasn't very fair."

I blinked slowly.

"So, think about it, okay? I mean, really think about it. I have to leave on Sunday, but—"

"Sunday?" I slapped his hand away from my mouth and almost cried the word. "But that's four days from now."

"I know." He took my hands again. "I wish I had more time but I need to go back home to do the paperwork and pack."

Four days.

He was going to *leave* in four days? We'd just started to build our relationship. *How could he go now? What would that mean for us? Could we survive such distance between us?*

But maybe we didn't have to. He said she could go with him.

My mind spun.

Could I really go to Africa? Just pack up and go? What about school? My family? My life?

I looked into Adam's beautiful green eyes.

But what about Adam? Would I be able to live without him if I stayed?

I loved him. There was no doubt about that. But would love be enough in a place like Africa?

"Hey." He must have seen the struggle in my eyes. "I know it's a lot."

"A real lot."

"Didn't really expect it would work out this way," he said. "And I really didn't expect that I would fall in love with the most amazing girl this summer."

"But it did."

"And I did."

I blinked hard, trying desperately *not* to cry. I knew he

was excited. This was what he wanted. I refused to make him feel bad when he should be happy for his future. I would not be the girl who begged and cried and tried to make him choose between the career that was so important to him, and me.

"So did I," I said with a small smile I didn't feel. "Fall in love, I mean."

He brushed his thumb along my bottom lip. "I knew what you meant." He kissed me. Soft and slow.

With his lips on mine, I forgot about the impossible decision in front of me, if only for a second. The only thing that mattered was Adam. Because, at least for the moment, we were together and everything was perfect.

"You really want me to come?"

His lips curled up, transforming his handsome face. "I really do. There are plenty of opportunities. It would be the most incredible experience. Think about the difference we could make together. All the people we could help. It would be unbelievable."

"It really would be amazing. But—"

"Don't answer me now." He pressed a finger to my lips. "I know it's a major decision and I've had months to think about it while I just sprang this on you." That was true. "Think about it," he said. "Talk to your family if you like."

There was *no* way I could do that. I knew exactly what they'd say. There was no way they'd be able to stay unbiased for such a decision.

Four days. Four days. How was I supposed to make such a major life decision in only four days? "I wish we had more time."

"I know." He pulled me close. "Me too. Let me take you to dinner on Friday," he said when he released me. "Tell me your decision then."

"Friday." I found myself nodding. "Okay."

"I promise, no matter what happens, Maureen, I will always love you."

Two Months Earlier

October

It wasn't very often that I was able to have my whole family in one place these days, even for a special occasion. Canadian Thanksgiving fell on the second weekend of October, and with the latest season of *Mr. Summer*, the television show that Gwen had sold based on her real-life personal blog and the events of her and Ian's life, done filming, most of the McCormick clan was still in town and had some free time.

The television show was a bit of a family affair, with Cal starring as his older brother, Ian. I worried that it would be a little strange for my youngest son, who was a mega celebrity in his own right, to play the role of his older brother, but it had worked out perfectly and Cal had even earned himself a few award nominations for his part.

Jade had taken a short maternity leave from working as the producer on the show when Clara was born but had quickly found some work/life balance by bringing the baby to work with her when Mitch had to teach his classes. The television show had turned into a phenomenon and had been renewed for another season, and I couldn't be prouder of all of them.

"It's so nice to have you all here," I said as we took our seats at the dining room table in my old house that Ian and Gwen now called their home. "Well, most of you," I added.

"Maybe we can FaceTime Amber and Cole later?" Gwen offered.

"Yes." I smiled. "I would like that. It's good that they went to see Cole's sister, but it would be nice if we were all here together."

"It would be," Cal said from the other end of the table. "Especially because we have something we want to say."

"Wait until everyone is sitting down at least." Milena chastised him, but there was a smile on her face as she stood to join him.

"What's going on?" Evie looked to Jade, who shrugged as she fastened a bib around Clara's neck.

The baby looked delighted to be sitting in her high chair at the dining room table, but less thrilled with the bib her mother was struggling to keep in place.

I pulled my attention from my granddaughter to my youngest son, who was grinning broadly.

"So tell us already," Mitch called out. "The turkey is getting cold."

Cal's mood wouldn't be dampened.

"You're having a baby!" Chelsea clapped her hands together.

"A baby?" I tried not to sound too hopeful. "Really?"

"No." Milena shook her head. "Sorry, Maureen. We're not pregnant."

"Then what?" Gwen tried and failed not to sound disappointed.

"We're getting married."

"When?"

"What?"

"Congratulations!"

Everyone started talking at once with Cal's announcement. But it was Ian who asked, "Are you even engaged?"

Milena giggled and shook her head a little before finally shrugging. "Yes and no. But it doesn't matter because we can't do anything the traditional way."

It was true. With Cal's superstardom, everything they did

was picked up on almost at once by the media and the paparazzi. Living in Cedar Springs gave them a little bit more privacy, but even then, the world seemed to be hungry for news about *Calina.*

"And that's why we're keeping this all a little hush-hush," Cal added. "It's also why we're going to have the ceremony on Christmas Eve."

I almost choked on the sip of water I'd just taken. "What? *This* Christmas?"

Milena nodded. "We thought it would be the best time to do it, when all the reporters should be home with their families and not expecting anything like a wedding."

"I don't think any of us were expecting a wedding at Christmas." Declan stood and gave his brother a hug. "Congratulations. I think it's fabulous."

"We all do," Gwen added. "And I agree with you. I think the timing is perfect."

I had to agree. The timing *was* perfect. Or it would have been except for the little trip I had planned to North Carolina the week before Christmas. A trip I hadn't yet told any of my children about.

"To the happy couple." I raised my glass. "It's going to be perfect."

We all toasted to Cal and Milena and began to pass around platters of food.

I only picked at my dinner, trying to work out in my head the logistics of traveling so far away, so close to both Christmas and now the wedding of my youngest son. The timing was already quite tight, but I'd managed to get some good flights that had me home late on the afternoon of the twentieth. It didn't leave a lot of room for error, or any disruptions, but it was the best I could do. And it should be enough time for everything.

"I have something I'd like to say, too." I tapped on my glass with a fork before I lost my nerve and changed my mind. It took a moment, but everyone quieted down and turned to look in my direction.

I dabbed at my lips with my napkin. "I have quite a bit to be thankful for this year. Having my family all together, with the exception of Amber and Cole, of course. And I'm especially thankful for my beautiful granddaughter."

Everyone murmured and nodded.

I took a sip of wine before continuing. "I have something else to be grateful for this year, too."

Declan winked in my direction. "What's that, Mom?"

I had a feeling he might already suspect what I was going to say.

"You all know that I've recently reconnected with Adam." More murmurs and a few giggles. "It's been really nice to get to know him again after all these years, and we've decided to meet in person."

"What?"

"That's great!"

"When?"

"Are you sure that's a good idea?"

"Cool."

The responses were as mixed as I'd expected when I decided to tell the children about my upcoming trip over their family dinner. I hadn't been expecting Cal and Milena's announcement, however, which was going to make the details of my trip an even bigger deal than I'd originally anticipated, planning it so close to Christmas.

I took a breath, put a smile on my face, and told them the details I'd previously arranged.

"Whoa." Ian was the first to protest, the way I knew he would. "You can't be serious." Out of all my boys, Ian had experienced most of the fallout from his father's betrayal all those years ago. He'd taken his role of the eldest very seriously and had become the *man of the house* at the tender age of eighteen. Although he'd been supportive when Declan had found Adam, he was still the most concerned about me.

He protected and looked out for me. It was sweet, really.

Only, I was a grown woman and didn't need protection.

"I'm very serious." I calmly reached for the jug of iced tea and poured myself a glass.

"You're going to travel across the continent to meet a man you only know through letters?" Ian shook his head. "Why is it that you haven't spoken on the phone? That's weird. You do know there's a thing called video chat, right?"

"It's not weird." I fixed my gaze on my eldest. "I've explained this before. We write letters because Adam is working in very remote parts of Africa. It's an easier and more reliable way to communicate. People have been writing letters back and forth for hundreds of years, Ian."

"I think it's sweet." Gwen gave me a wink. "Very romantic."

"It is ridiculous." Mitch was the next to object. He set his cutlery down and folded his hands over his plate. "The entire world is connected," he continued. "There's no reason you have to be so old-fashioned."

"I happen to like being old-fashioned."

It *was* true that letter writing had its drawbacks, but I'd grown to enjoy it and look forward to the letters. I agreed with Gwen. It was very romantic. Every day, I was excited to check the mailbox and my heart would skip a beat, just as it had when I was a girl, when I saw the envelope with the familiar handwriting. And with the letters, unlike with email, there was no pressure to respond immediately. Instead, I had time to read and reread each letter and carefully think about the response before sitting down to write my own letter. Somehow, it had felt a lot more natural the way we were doing it.

"I don't like it." Ian shook his head. "What do we really know about this guy, Mom?"

I almost choked on my iced tea. "Excuse me?"

"What are his intentions?"

Intentions?

"Mom, at your age—"

"Enough." I pushed up from my chair, put both hands on the table, and glared at my son. "First of all, I do not appreciate your tone, young man."

Ian opened his mouth to protest the way I addressed him, but fortunately for him, had the good sense to close it again.

"Second, Adam is a few years older than me. And he is *not* old. Nor am I." I waited for Ian to acknowledge me with a quick nod. "I assure you I have plenty of life left in me, son, and part of that life is going to involve reuniting with an old friend, which frankly, is none of your business." I looked around the table at each of them in turn. "I do apologize if I gave any of you the impression that I was looking for your opinion on the matter. I am not."

I didn't make a habit of raising my voice at my children. I never had, even when they were a pack of rambunctious boys trying every one of my last nerves. So when I did, it had the desired impact. Ian and Mitch, particularly, looked properly chastised.

After a moment, I took my seat and, with a shaking hand, took a sip of my iced tea.

"Okay." Declan stood up from his spot at the table. "I think Mom's made her point." He smiled in my direction. "And it's a good one. I would just like to add that Adam Lancaster is a respected optometrist who has a very successful practice on the East Coast. He's spent most of his career traveling to impoverished countries to provide free optical care for people in need, only returning to Canada and his practice to raise more funds for his charitable work. He's dedicated his life to his philanthropic causes." He offered me a supportive smile. "But most importantly, he's an old friend of our mother's, and I don't see any reason why we shouldn't all be anything less than supportive."

I let my shoulders relax, as the tension I'd been holding in them released a little. "Thank you, Dec."

He nodded and gave me a wink before returning to his seat. Evie looked at him adoringly and squeezed his hand.

At least I had the support of two of them.

"It's not that I'm not supportive, Mom." Cal cleared his throat. "But I do have to ask, were we the only ones who noticed the dates? Do you really have to go at Christmas time, Mom? That's the wedding."

"It's also Clara's first Christmas, Mom." Mitch raised an eyebrow.

"I'll be back for the wedding," I assured Cal first. "I wouldn't miss your special day for anything." I directed my last comment to Milena, who did not look reassured at all. "And of course, I wouldn't dream of missing my granddaughter's first Christmas. You all are worrying over nothing. I'll be gone for a few days and back on the twentieth."

"That's cutting it pretty close, Mom."

I didn't disagree with Cal, but there was nothing I could do about the timing.

"The plans are already made." I picked up my fork and knife and sliced into the turkey on my plate. "I wasn't actually asking anybody for their permission."

I didn't lift my head to make eye contact, but I didn't miss the chuckle from Declan's direction and the sigh from Ian's. They could think what they wanted to. I was a grown woman, and I didn't need my children's approval to do anything, especially when my children were acting as if I were completely incapable of caring for myself.

As far as I was concerned, the subject was closed.

After a few minutes of silence, Chelsea changed the subject easily by asking Milena questions about the upcoming wedding. Soon, conversations sprang up all around me, and my announcement was forgotten.

It wasn't until later when I was cleaning up in the kitchen that my impending trip came up again.

"I'm sorry, Mom." Ian, a stack of plates in his hand, joined me at the sink. "I don't mean to give you such a hard time," he continued. "I'm just concerned is all."

"I know you are."

"I can't help it that I'm a little protective over you."

I tipped my head and examined my eldest before pulling my hands out of the soapy water and drying them on a nearby towel. I knew all too well the extra responsibility Ian felt over me. I'd often wondered whether maybe I should have dated more, or let someone else into my life in order to take some of the pressure off Ian. But I had been gone for so many years, and I would never expose them to a string of men. They might have been adults now, but they had been my world all my life and they still were. I would never sacrifice that. Ian was a good son, and as far as I was concerned, he was a happy and healthy man with the love of a great woman, and they were welcoming children into their family. He didn't need to worry about me.

Love wasn't in the cards for everyone. I'd resigned myself to that many years earlier. Even before Harold's betrayal was made public. I couldn't imagine trying again with anyone new.

Anyone but Adam.

"So, he's an optometrist," Ian said, bringing me back to the moment. "What else should we know about this man?" He held up a hand. "And before you get mad again, I'm only asking because I should have asked a long time ago when Declan gave you the letter. I swear I won't try to stop you, but it's long past time I asked some questions. Besides, I think it's fair that I should have some of the information." He winked. "You know, just in case."

"In case I get abducted?" I laughed at the absurdity of it but resigned myself to telling him what I could. "Adam and I met a very long time ago." I began to tell him the story, leaving out most of the romantic details.

"So, he was your boyfriend?"

I squeezed my eyes shut for a moment. I'd never discussed such things with my boys before. It felt, odd, to say the least. Particularly considering it had been almost forty years since I and Adam had even seen each other.

"We didn't really use those kinds of labels back then." I skirted the question easily and moved on. "I had just graduated from high school and was excited about the future in front of me, and he was on his way to Africa to save the world."

"It sounds like he's still doing that."

"It sure does." I smiled to myself. I'd been so pleased to hear that for all these years, Adam had been making the difference he'd always hoped he would. "And when he's not in Africa, he's got a practice out East in Northern Ontario."

"So if he was your boyfriend but he ended up going to Africa…" Ian raised his eyebrows.

I shot him a look, and he pressed his lips together instead of offering up a comment.

"As I said, we didn't use those labels. But basically, at the end of the summer, he went to Africa, and I…" I gazed past Ian, out to the mountains before answering. "I met your father."

"Do you mean to tell me that this mystery Adam could have been my father if—"

"No." I stopped him from going any further.

"Really? Because I'm kind of getting the impression that maybe you and Adam—"

"Wanted different things. I'd just graduated from high

school, and I was looking forward to going to college and experiencing everything that came along with that." I smiled at the memory of my eighteen-year-old self, so full of possibility and hope. "He was older, recently graduated from college, and knew exactly what he wanted out of life already." I shrugged as casually as I could. "The timing wasn't right."

It was the same thing I'd told Declan when he, too, had asked why I and Adam hadn't worked out. In fact, I'd told myself that very thing so many times over the years that, for a time, I'd even started to believe it.

Ian nodded as if he understood. "That makes sense."

It didn't.

It never had.

"You had to make a choice."

I nodded sadly. "I did."

"And you chose your future," Ian said matter-of-factly. "That makes sense."

I closed my eyes and inhaled deeply before responding. "That's just it," I said when I opened my eyes again. "I didn't."

Chapter Seven

Present

ELISE'S HEAD was pressed back into the headrest, my eyes closed when I finished telling her about my children's reaction. I sat for a moment, sure that the older woman had fallen asleep.

"Why did you stop?" The older woman's eyes snapped open. "You're just getting to the good part."

"The good part?" I shook my head. "I thought you were sleeping."

"I was resting my eyes. At my age, they get tired of looking at things all the time."

I raised an eyebrow in surprise.

"And yes, the good part," Elise said again. "The part of the story that brought us here to today. Obviously you told him no. You broke the poor boy's heart and sent him to Africa alone."

I had to chuckle at Elise's certainty. "Well, if you know how it ends already, why are you asking?"

Elise shook her head and picked up her crochet. "I don't know how it ends. No one does. Not even you."

"I do know."

"No. You don't." The old woman's hand stopped moving, and she stared at me. "Because if you did, you wouldn't be here, waiting for him to walk through that door." She gestured with her head toward the door that, no matter how many times it had opened and closed as guests braved the blizzard to go next door to the pub, hadn't produced Adam.

"I'm not—"

"You are."

I blew out a breath. "Okay, I am," I admitted. "I can't help it. But yes, I am hoping for some sort of a miracle that the roads opened and Adam is on his way."

"Because you don't know the end of the story yet."

"I guess I don't," I reluctantly agreed. "But I don't think he's coming." It was a thought I hadn't wanted to speak out loud. Even before the storm, I'd worried he wouldn't come. It wasn't completely rational, but there was part of me that couldn't help but think that he'd changed his mind.

"Why would you think that?"

I shrugged. "Do you think that sometimes history repeats itself?"

"Sometimes, certainly. But I don't think that's the case here."

"I haven't finished telling you what happened." My smile was sad, and I looked down at my hands. "The end of—" I caught myself. "Well, I guess it's not the end, not yet," I added. "It's just what happened next."

"Exactly." Elise nodded in agreement.

"What about you? Do you know the end of your story?"

I regretted the question as soon as it slipped from my mouth and Elise's face fell.

"I'm sorry," I said quickly. "You don't have to answer—"

"No. It's fine. We're sharing stories, and I'm happy enough

to share all of mine. As it turns out, I do know the end of my story."

Judging by her face, I assumed it wasn't a happy one. "I'm sorry."

"For what?"

"That you didn't get your happy ending."

The skin around Elise's eyes crinkled as a mischievous grin took over her features. "Who said I didn't?"

I leaned forward in my seat, eager to hear the rest of my new friend's story. "What happened? I don't understand. Alex was married and—"

"It wasn't a happy time." Elise grew serious. "Cancer is an awful thing."

My heart fell, and I knew at once what had happened.

"You see, despite my private feelings, I'd grown to love Alex's family as if they were my own. They were married forty years when Alex was widowed."

"Oh." My hand fluttered to my chest. "That is awful."

Elise nodded. "It was hard on everyone. Especially Susan. She had only just married herself. Such a tender time to lose a parent."

"I can't imagine how hard that must have been on everyone." I reached across the distance for Elise's hand. "And you."

I smiled sadly. "I grieved in my own way, but I did my best to be there for them both. We'd always remained close. The best of friends." I smiled with a private memory. "And over time…when Alex was ready…"

"You were together?"

The older woman smiled, and I caught a glimpse of what a beauty she must have been when she was younger. I radiated with happiness and joy. "The love between us never died and after all those years, things had changed, and it was a different time. Our relationship was more accepted by then. And for those who didn't accept it, we didn't care. We were in love, and the universe had conspired for us to finally be together. When Alex was widowed, it really hit home for us—life is short. There isn't any time to waste."

It was easy to see the love on Elise's face, and I could feel my new friend's happiness radiating. "You got your happy ending. How excellent." I clasped my hands together and smiled. A moment later, that smile slid from my face when Elise spoke again.

"Oh dear, I never said that was the ending. It was only the next chapter."

"Do you ever regret the way things happened?"

Elise didn't hesitate in her answer. "Not for a second. Our story wouldn't have been the same had we been together all those years ago, and we would never have had Susan. I don't regret anything."

That was a good way to be.

I thought about my own life for a moment. There had been times over the years when I'd wondered what it would have been like if things had gone differently, but that was normal. And after Harold left, maybe I could have looked up Adam then or tried dating other men. But I wasn't ready. I needed to spend some time seeing the last of my boys raised and out of the house and then focusing on myself. If life had turned out differently, if I'd ended up going to Africa with Adam, I wouldn't have my four boys and my wonderful daughters. There wouldn't be little Clara and so many other grandbabies I knew I would have in the coming years.

I would have missed out on so much life. And what a wonderful life it was.

"I don't regret anything either. Life has a way of working out the way it's supposed to."

"And is Adam supposed to walk in that door tonight?"

The question startled me. I was saved from answering it when Elise spoke again.

"Why don't you tell me what happened when you met Adam for dinner? How did you tell him that you couldn't go with him?"

"That's just the thing." I sank into my chair with a sigh and let my head drop back. "I didn't."

Thirty-Seven Years Ago

Time seemed to speed up in the days since Adam announced he'd been accepted into the program that would take him to Africa. I spent most of my time staring at the clock, wishing for time to slow down. I needed more time.

It was an impossible decision to make.

Especially considering it was one that I had never dreamed of. My whole life, there was one path. I would go to college and earn a diploma or certificate in business administration or education or nursing. While I was there, I would meet a nice boy from a good family with excellent job prospects and we'd get engaged. Probably in my senior year because it was important for me to finish my education, even if I wasn't sure about what kind of career I might actually want to have.

We'd marry in the summer after graduation and settle down in a little house not *too* far from where I grew up. My best friend Sue Ann would move in next door, or maybe down the street so they weren't too close, and then I and my new husband would start a family. I wanted lots of children. Three girls and three boys. I would spend my days baking cupcakes and helping with homework. When the children were older, maybe I'd go back to work part-time or find a charity I was interested in supporting.

And every summer, I would take my little family to the lake, where we would spend our summers.

It was the only life I'd ever dreamed of. It would be a quiet and happy life.

In all my daydreams, I had never one time dreamed of leaving my family and friends, abandoning my education, and moving to Africa. Not once.

Adam told me to think about it before I answered him, and that's exactly what I did. It was *all* I'd done after leaving him that night. I barely slept and after the second night, I woke early to ask my mother for her car keys before my sister got the chance. And without even eating breakfast, I was gone so I could be at the Cedar Springs public library before the doors even opened.

For a town so small, the library was surprisingly well stocked and the librarian was eager to help in my *research project.* "I need everything you have on Africa," I told the portly woman whose glasses continually slid down her nose. "Especially anything recent, like a magazine article or newspaper story."

"Absolutely. What part of Africa are you interested in specifically?"

The question jolted me. "What part?"

"Yes. What part of Africa? Is there a country specifically that you're interested in? It's quite a large continent."

I felt the flush wash over my cheeks. In all of my conversations with Adam, I had never asked him what country he would be going to. But there was a flash of memory. "I think maybe South Africa. But could we maybe start with a bit of everything? Would that work?"

"Absolutely." The librarian shoved her glasses up her nose. "Let me see what I can find for you to get started."

I spent most of the day at a table in the back of the library, reading every single thing I could find about *Africa.* I read about the wild animals, the different tribes that occupied various regions, and the bigger cities like Johannesburg. I scanned articles about civil unrest and wars. I learned about the independence of many of Africa's nations and the political changes. And when I was done learning everything I possibly could about a part of the world that still seemed so wild and foreign to me, I left the library and walked down to the lakefront.

I wasn't sure what my research would reveal, but on some level, deep down, I'd been hoping for some nugget of information that might make my decision obvious. But ultimately, there was nothing in any of those books or news articles that could have helped me make up my mind.

Choosing Adam would mean giving up everything I'd ever known. My family, friends, and home. College and my dreams for the future.

It was unthinkable.

But so was not choosing Adam.

It was both an impossible decision and an easy one.

I knew what I had to do even though it would break my heart in a million different ways. There was only one choice.

I walked to the end of the beach and found an old log to sit on. I pulled up my legs and rested my head on my knees. I sat that way for hours, staring out at the lake until finally, it was time to go home and get ready to meet Adam for our dinner date so I could give him my decision.

We'd agreed to meet at the restaurant. A quiet bistro set back from the busier Main Street, with candles and fresh flowers on every table. It was romantic and intimate and absolutely the perfect place for me to tell Adam of my decision. My body vibrated with nerves. After tonight, everything would change and as much as I wasn't quite ready for that change, I knew there'd be no going back from it.

"Right this way." The hostess greeted me and led me to the table in the back of the restaurant. "I'm afraid your date isn't here yet, but can I get you something while you wait?"

I took my seat and smiled at the woman. "Two glasses of lemonade, please." I ordered what had become *our* drink. Ever since the night of the summer solstice dance when Adam had bought me a glass of lemonade and changed my summer. And my life. "I'm sure he'll be here any moment."

The drink was cold and tangy on my lips. I sipped it slowly and mentally prepared myself for what I was going to tell Adam. There'd been no doubt in my mind about what I had to do. It sent a cacophony of nerves and excitement through me that made it almost impossible to sit still, but I was one hundred percent sure of my decision. I was going to go to Africa with Adam.

And I couldn't wait to tell him.

My drink was almost empty when the waiter came by to check on me. "You are still waiting for one more?"

"I am." My cheeks heated with a blush. "I'm sure he's just running a little bit late. What time is it, please?"

"It's quarter past six," the waiter offered. "Could I get you a refill?" He gestured to my almost empty glass, but I shook my head.

"No. Thank you. I'll wait until he gets here. I'm sure he'll be along any minute."

"I'm sure he will be."

I didn't miss the way the waiter looked at me with just the slightest bit of pity on his features. He thought I'd been stood up. But he didn't know Adam the way I did. The waiter had no idea that we were about to go to Africa together and start a life full of adventure and excitement. Adam would never stand me up. He loved me.

Still, the worry started to niggle at the back of my brain as I considered the options that might have kept Adam from being on time. He would never be late on purpose. All summer, he'd been early for our dates. Picking me up at least ten minutes before our agreed-upon time.

Something must have happened. *Maybe a flat tire?* I wouldn't let my mind travel to anything worse, and there was no way I would entertain the idea that Adam would stand me up. It wasn't a possibility. Especially on such an important night.

Still, as I looked across the table at his empty seat and his glass of lemonade with the ice cubes long since melted, beads of water sweating on the side of the glass, a sense of dread settled over me.

When I couldn't stand it a moment longer, I pushed back my chair and was about to go in search of the hostess to see whether I could use their house phone when the waiter once more reappeared.

His face was set in a thin line as he handed me an envelope. "This was delivered for you."

"Who delivered it?" Fear raced through my veins. I craned my head, trying to see the front door and who might have delivered the envelope the waiter still held in his hand. I refused to take it. Afraid of what it might contain.

"Miss." The waiter shook the envelope, and when I still wouldn't take it, he set it on the table in front of me. "If there's anything else I can get you…"

His words trailed away. I couldn't focus on anything else except the envelope in front of me, and my name written in Adam's precise handwriting.

He wasn't coming.

I felt it in my gut before I even picked up the envelope. Somehow, I managed to stuff the offending paper in my purse, put a few dollars on the table, and walk out of the restaurant with my head held high. It felt like everyone was looking at me.

My heart was breaking in a million pieces before I got to the beach and the log where I'd sat only a few hours ago. It was only then that I pulled out the piece of paper and read Adam's note.

Dearest Maureen,

Words will never be able to properly express how much I care about you. As you know, I never expected to fall in love this summer. I never expected you. Some of the very best things in life are unplanned. And you are one of the very best things in my life, Maureen. That is what makes this so hard.

I would love nothing more than for you to come to Africa with me. Together, I know we would make such a difference where it really matters, and we would never have to feel the pain of saying goodbye.

If I know you the way I think I do, Maureen, I know you agree with me. I know you will say yes to me so we can leave together. And that's why I couldn't meet you for dinner tonight. Selfishly, I want nothing more than to walk hand in hand with you into the greatest adventure of our lives. But I cannot.

I love you too much to let you come with me. I know you dream of getting married and having a family of your own. And you will be the most amazing mother. I cannot let you give that up for me and my dreams. I know in my heart that I will not be able to give you what you need and desire so much out of life. I wouldn't be able to live with myself if I knew that you'd given up what you want most in life for me.

Please forgive me for my cowardice, Maureen. It

breaks my heart to know that by the time you read this I will already be gone and I will not be able to say goodbye properly, but I fear I'm not strong enough to walk away from you.

You deserve to be happy. Happier than I will ever be able to make you.

If only we had met at another time or place, maybe it could have been different, but I will never regret meeting you or having the most wonderful summer.

I will think of you often.

Forever and Always,
Your Adam

A Few Days Earlier

December

I'd been packed for three days already.

It had been a long time since I had taken a trip, and even longer since I'd had to use my passport. I'd had to double-check that it hadn't expired. It hadn't. And the passport now sat atop my printed flight itinerary, the reservation confirmation, and the instructions on how to meet the shuttle that would take me from the airport to the Merry Falls Inn in the mountains of North Carolina once I arrived.

Declan was due to arrive in twenty minutes to drive me to the airport.

There was one more thing I needed.

In my bedroom, I pulled a shoebox off the top shelf of my closet and sat with it on the bed. Inside, there was a selection of items from over the years, including the hospital bracelets from when each of my boys were born, various newspaper clippings of important events, including my marriage announcement to Harold. And underneath everything, the first letter I'd ever received from Adam.

Even after all these years, I'd only ever read it one time. But I still remembered every word.

If only we had met at another time or place.

We were about to do that. A different time. A different place.

Would it be different?

What if he stood me up again?

I had never felt grief the way I had after Adam left. I'd taken to my bed for days until my mother finally forcibly made me get up because we were returning to the city. For weeks after school started, I walked around in a daze, unable to process the fact that he'd left for Africa without me.

At first, Sue Ann encouraged me to ask Adam's aunt and uncle for his contact information so I might write to him, but I couldn't bring myself to do so. "He doesn't want me."

"He doesn't want you to give up your future," Sue Ann would tell me over and over. "It's different. He loves you."

"It doesn't matter."

And it didn't. He was gone. After a few months, the pain lessened. I reluctantly let Sue Ann drag me to parties and dances on campus. Somehow the years went by and eventually I met Harold and the rest of my life fell into place.

I took the letter and slipped it into my purse with the other, more recent letters from Adam. A moment later, there was a knock on my door.

"Come in, Dec. I'm almost ready to go," I said as the door opened behind me.

"That's good. But I'm not Declan."

I spun around to see my youngest son.

"Some would say I'm far more handsome." Cal grinned cheekily.

"You're all very handsome." I greeted him with a kiss on my cheek. "This is a nice surprise. I wasn't expecting you today."

"I wanted to make sure I saw you before you left." Cal dropped his head, and I could see there was something on his mind.

"What's going on? Is it Milena? Is everything okay for the wedding?"

"Oh yes. She's fine. Milena's great, actually. We're so excited, and I don't think the media has any idea about the wedding, which is exactly what we wanted. You know how they can be."

I laughed. "I've definitely seen it, yes. You two are making an excellent decision to have a small, intimate ceremony. It will be beautiful. And I won't miss it for anything, Cal. You know that, right? That's not why you're here, is it? I told you I would—"

"No, Mom. I know you won't miss it." He took a step forward and put his hand on my arm. "I'm here because I couldn't let you leave without telling you how sorry I am."

"You have nothing to be sorry for." I tried to laugh, but Cal wasn't smiling.

"Seriously, Mom. I really am sorry, for all of us." He shrugged. "Except maybe Declan." It was only then he smiled. "We haven't been very supportive about all this, and I think that's actually really shitty of us. Sorry," he added quickly. "Crappy."

"No," I said as seriously as I could. "I think shitty is a much better word for how you've all been behaving."

He cracked a smile, and I shook my head before pulling my

youngest son in for a hug. "You have nothing to apologize for. I know this must all be very strange for you boys. For all those years, I never dated and—"

"That's just it, Mom. You never dated. And you should have. If you wanted to, that is. We just want you to be happy, Mom. You've given all of us so much. It's because of you that we've all been able to find the loves of our lives."

"No, Cal. It's not because of me. It's because you are all amazing men with so much to offer. That is why you attracted such amazing women."

Cal flashed the smile that made him famous. "And why do you think we all grew up to be the men we are, Mom?"

He waited for an answer he didn't get. Instead, I shook my head and chuckled. "Thank you, Cal. It means a lot that you stopped by."

"I just wanted to make sure you know, Mom. Mitch and Ian support you, too. Even if they have a harder time showing it. It's only because Ian thinks he needs to be responsible for us all in some weird way, and I think Mitch is just so wrapped up in his own brand-new family that he forgets sometimes that it's okay for the rest of us to have things going on. I think he's worried that you're going to run off with this guy and miss Clara's first Christmas." He shrugged. "I mean, it's not like she'll remember it."

"I assure you that I'm not going to run off with anyone, and I will not miss Clara's first Christmas, or your wedding. I promise." I held my arms out for another hug right as there was another knock on the door, followed by Declan.

"Are we all ready to go?"

I pulled away from my youngest son's embrace and smiled at Declan. "I'm so ready."

"Remember, Mom," Cal said a few minutes later as we were loading my bag in the back of Declan's car. "Don't fall in love and run off with this guy."

"No way, Mom." I was about to speak when Declan interrupted. "Fall in love if that's what you want to do." Cal looked like he was going to protest, but Declan focused on me. "A very wise woman told me once that it was never too late for love."

I smiled to myself. I'd fallen in love with Adam years ago, and I wasn't entirely sure I'd ever stopped loving him.

"But maybe don't run away with him, though, okay?" Declan added, making them all laugh.

Chapter Eight

Present

ELISE LOOKED tired by the time I was done telling my story. I glanced at the time and realized with a shock that we'd been sitting and chatting for hours. "I've kept you too long," I told Elise. "I should probably let you get to bed."

Elise sat up straight. "Did I say I was tired?"

"No, but—"

"I haven't finished telling you my own story. Unless, of course, you don't want the sad details on how it ends."

My face twisted in concern. "Why would it be sad? A good love story should always have a happy ending."

"Ahh." Elise's smile was so sad it almost broke my heart. "That's where most people get it wrong. There is no happily ever after. That's a myth. I presume people tell each other that because the alternative is just too depressing."

"Elise." I leaned forward in my chair and reached across the space between us. "I don't understand. You and Alex...you said you were able to be together in the end. That's a good thing."

"It was a good thing." She nodded. "And make no mistake, all the years before that, they were good, too. Just because we were not lovers does not mean my life and heart were not very full by having Alex and all of them in my life the way I did." She closed her eyes for a moment. "But nothing lasts forever, Maureen. Alex and I were together. But by then we were over seventy, and life has a way of catching up to you sooner or later."

I blinked back the tears that sprang to my eyes, but Elise continued.

"We were very happy for a time. By then Susan and her new husband were running things at the family business, and I'd retired from my job as well." There was a hint of a smile on her face. "We had a cute little cottage close to the ocean," she continued. "We spent our days walking the beach, reading books and playing cards. We both loved to cook, and we had so much fun working our way through cookbooks, trying out new recipes."

"It sounds lovely." I couldn't help but think how nice it would be to have that kind of love and companionship in my own life. My thoughts went to Adam. *Would he like to do those things with me? Would we have a chance at that kind of companionship?*

I pushed the thoughts away to listen to the rest of my new friend's story.

"You always think you'll have time," Elise said. "That's a lie. It only took a few years for the cancer to take hold."

I'd suspected it was coming, but still, I gasped. "I'm sorry."

Elise acknowledged me with a nod. "It wasn't a kind disease. But cancer never is." She took a shuddering breath as she recalled a memory. "In the end, I'm thankful that I was there with her. I held her hand and eased her way from this world as she took her last breath. No one else could have done it."

"That must have been so hard. I'm so sorry, Elise."

A small tear slipped down the older woman's cheek, and it was only then that I registered what Elise had just said.

"Alex. Alex was a—"

Elise nodded. "As I said, it was a different time. We never could have been together." A smile crept across her face. "From the moment I met Alexandra, I knew she would change my life. She was my lover, my best friend, the mother of the little girl who became the light of my own life, and eventually, she became my wife. We were married before she passed. We had eight amazing years together. I wouldn't have traded it for anything. The world truly has come a long way."

I squeezed Elise's hand gently before releasing it again and sitting back in my chair. "It really has." I shook my head and took a moment to absorb everything Elise had been through. "I'm sorry your story had to end that way and you didn't have more time."

"Oh, like I said, dear. There is no such thing as a happy ever after. Just happy for right now. And I've been *so* happy. We never know how much time we will have. So be happy. Be happy now, with whatever that looks like and whatever life gives you."

"That's good advice."

"Damn straight it is."

I laughed.

"Maybe that happiness is with your Adam?" Her smile was mischievous but my faded.

I'd always wished that Adam would be my happy ever after. Or, as Elise had put it, happy for right now. Either way, on some level, I had to admit that for most of my life, I had secretly thought of Adam as my *one*.

But what if he wasn't?

What if, after all this time and years of wondering, never mind the last few months when I'd secretly hoped that maybe now, maybe finally, it *was* our time…what if he didn't come?

What then?

"He'll be here." Elise spoke without opening her eyes, reading my mind.

"But the storm…"

"He'll be here."

Before I could speak again, or protest that the storm was too intense, there was a ruckus at the front desk, followed by the front door of the inn opening with a rush of wind and snow, along with two heavily bundled individuals covered in a layer of snow.

I rose from my chair and took a tentative step toward the commotion. *Adam?* It couldn't be. Or could it?

Through all the layers of clothing and snow, it was impossible to tell who the individuals were. Even if I knew what Adam looked like after all this time, there wouldn't be any way to know whether he was one of the new arrivals. *Yet…*

I took another step forward and then another.

Behind me, I was certain I'd heard Elise say, "I told you he'd come."

But it wasn't until one of the snow-covered individuals turned to face me and pulled off his knit cap that I knew for sure. Adam's green eyes, set in a familiar, but older face, looked directly at me. His smile widened as he searched the room, his gaze finally landing on me.

"Maureen." He shook his head a little, as if he couldn't believe it was her. "Sorry I'm late."

He looked so different. But at the same time, he looked exactly the same.

"Adam."

I stepped closer, Elise and the conversation we'd been having completely forgotten. My only focus was on the man in front of me. *He'd come.* He'd made it through the storm. He hadn't stood me up. Again.

"How did…" I shook my head and tried again. "They said…" Words continued to fail me. "But the roads are…"

"The roads are closed." He chuckled a little and brushed snow from his jacket. "Trust me. They are very closed. I'd only made it to the turn-off from the highway when I ran into the closure. They told me there was no way I would make it up here tonight."

"But here you are."

"Here I am." His grin grew even wider, if it were possible. "Nothing was going to keep me from meeting you tonight, Maureen." Adam's face got suddenly serious. "I made that mistake once before. I was not going to stand you up again."

My stomach fluttered like I was eighteen again. Before I could ask any more questions, the other snow-covered man approached us.

A big man, with a frost-covered beard and a cap pulled low on his head. His eyes sparkled with life and despite his imposing size, I could see he was a jolly man. "Sorry to interrupt," he said with a slap on Adam's shoulder. "This must be—"

"This is Maureen." Adam introduced her. "Maureen, this is Kevin, the man responsible for getting me up to the inn tonight on his snowmobile in what can only be described as—"

"An impossible scenario." Kevin laughed. "It's a good thing I enjoy a challenge."

"A snowmobile?" That would explain the amount of snow covering both the men. "But…why? I mean…"

"When Adam here explained to me how important it was that he get up the mountain tonight, there was no way I could refuse." Kevin spoke matter-of-factly. "Besides, it was just a little snow."

"A little snow?" Lucy Gibbons appeared behind them, a

scowl on her face as she took in the amount of snow the men were dropping on the floor. "Can I please take your coats, gentlemen? I'm sure you're going to want a chance to warm up for a few minutes before we discuss the accommodation situation."

"Don't worry about me, Lucy. My buddy Russ works out here in maintenance. I can crash on his couch tonight and head back down to town in the morning."

The innkeeper nodded. "If that's okay with Russ, it's okay with us. But please do not risk your life again to head back down until it's safe."

The big man shrugged off the concern. "Just because the plows can't get through doesn't mean I'll be stopped." He laughed while Lucy shook her head.

"At any rate, thank you, for delivering Mr. Lancaster to us. It was incredibly dangerous, but—"

"Worth the risk." Adam looked directly at me. His green eyes flashed, and I couldn't help but blush a little.

I really did feel like a girl again.

Kevin laughed and slapped his thigh. "See?" he said to Lucy. "It was worth it." He turned to Adam and once more slapped him on the back. "Enjoy your stay, buddy. It was nice to meet you and hear all about your lady here."

By now, I was sure my face was on fire.

"Hold on, Kevin." Adam reached into the inner pocket of his thick jacket and pulled out his wallet before shrugging out of his jacket and handing it to the innkeeper. "I need to square up with you."

"Your money is no good with me." The other man held out his hand and shook his head. "Merry Christmas. I'm just happy I could be a small part of your story."

"Kevin. I told you I'd pay you. I—"

"I won't accept it." He crossed his arms and grinned. "Merry Christmas. To both of you." He nodded in my direction and added, "He was very determined to get up here tonight. I think he really likes you."

"Okay. Kevin, that's enough. Stop dripping all over my floor." Lucy Gibbons grabbed his arm and began to drag him away.

"Have fun, you two," Kevin called as the innkeeper dragged him away.

I watched him go and took the chance to compose myself before facing Adam. "He seems like quite the character."

Adam laughed. "That's putting it mildly. I met him in a pub in town, and when he heard my story…well, I guess *our* story…he insisted on helping me out." Adam's face turned serious. "And I'm really glad he did." He reached for my hand. "It's…well, it's incredible to see you again, Maureen. You look every bit as beautiful as you were when you were eighteen. More so."

"Thank you." I looked down at my hand in his and closed my eyes for a brief moment, unsure I could trust what I was seeing and feeling. "It is absolutely incredible to see you, Adam. I didn't…I wasn't sure… Well, I didn't think you were coming," I finished honestly.

"I'll admit, the weather is not ideal."

"It wasn't just the weather." There was no point beating around the bush. "I worried that maybe you might have changed your mind."

"Never."

He looked so sincere, any doubts I had vanished.

"Nothing was going to keep me away, Maureen. I've waited an entire lifetime to see you again."

My heart fluttered, just like it had all those years ago when he bought me that very first lemonade.

Remembering myself, I shook my head. "You must be freezing. Let me get you a tea or a hot chocolate. It's absolutely delicious here. And maybe we should see about your room." It occurred to me that earlier I'd been told that all the rooms at the inn were full because of the storm, and Lucy Gibbons mentioned there being a situation with the accommodations, too. "I think they might have given away your—"

"Maureen?" Adam caught my hand in his and held me back from heading to the front desk.

My breath caught in my throat, and I had to remind myself to breathe as he slowly tugged until I turned around to face him.

"Would it be too forward if I hugged you right now?"

The smile split my face and warmth rushed through me. "Not at all."

The moment I was in his arms, my body and my heart remembered, and the years melted away. I closed my eyes and took a deep breath, letting myself relax into his embrace.

The hug was unhurried and everything about it felt *right*. Adam pulled away too soon for my liking, but I was mollified when he took my hand and squeezed. "Now, what was this about a hot chocolate?"

With his hand still in mine, I turned to lead Adam toward the fireplace to introduce him to Elise. "She is just the sweetest woman with such an amazing story," I told Adam. "We spent the evening talking, and I think she'd really like to meet you."

But when I got close enough, I could see that Elise was gone. My crochet bag with the unfinished blanket I'd been working on sat on the floor. "She must have…" I turned in a circle, but there was no trace of the older woman. "I'll take her bag to the front desk and be right back with some hot chocolate."

Adam tugged my hand a little to keep me from going right away. "I'll be waiting right here."

He looked directly into my eyes, and my heart flipped. I didn't think it was possible to feel such a reaction from a man at my age. But then again, it wasn't just any man making me feel this way. It was Adam.

My Adam.

I smiled broadly. "I'll be right back."

I hurried to the front desk with the crochet bag.

"I'm sure you are." I handed the bag across the counter. "The older woman I was sitting with…in all the commotion, I didn't realize she'd excused herself."

"I'm sure you are." I handed the bag across the counter. "The older woman I was sitting with…in all the commotion, I didn't realize she'd excused herself."

"Oh yes, Elise. She retired to her room for the evening."

I felt a twinge of guilt for not saying goodnight after the lovely evening we'd shared. But somehow I was sure that Elise would approve of my distraction. "She must have left her crochet bag when she left," I said. "I wouldn't want it to get lost."

"Of course." Lucy smiled with a nod. "I'll be sure she gets it. And I will be sure to let you know when I have a solution to the room situation. In the meantime, please feel free to have a late dinner on the house. Just charge it to your room, and I'll be sure to take care of it."

"Thank you. That's very generous."

"It's the least we can do under the circumstances."

It was clear from the concerned look on the innkeeper's face that the room situation might be a little harder to solve than she was letting on. But I wasn't worried. Adam was here. He'd made it. He hadn't stood me up. For the moment, that was all that mattered. We'd figure out the rest later.

"Thank you. I'm sure a hot meal would be appreciated after his journey. And you'll make sure Elise gets her crocheting back? I know she wanted to finish the blanket."

"Of course, Mrs. McCormick." The young woman's smile was friendly. "Please let us know if there's anything else we can help you with."

I turned and looked at Adam, who was warming his hands by the fire. "I think I have everything I need now."

Chapter Nine

Present

A FEW MINUTES LATER, Adam decided to forgo the hot chocolate and opt for a warm dinner instead. We were seated in the hotel restaurant that was decorated for the holiday season just as nicely as the rest of the inn.

With the snowstorm still raging outside, candles on the table and the smell of pine mingling with the delicious aromas coming from the kitchen, and Adam sitting across from me, I was very cozy.

"I still can't believe you're here." I shook my head and sipped at the glass of wine I'd ordered. I rarely indulged these days, but reuniting with Adam was the most special occasion I could imagine.

"I told you, I wouldn't have missed this." He reached across the table, and I let him take my hands in his. His skin was still cool, but the moment he touched me, there was nothing but heat. "But maybe I can see how you might think I wouldn't come." His gaze dropped. "And I don't mean because of the storm."

"It did cross my mind," I admitted. "I feel like maybe this question is almost forty years too late, but I'm going to ask it anyway." Talking to Elise had helped me remember that there was no time to waste in this life. Not anymore. And as far as I was concerned, there was no point in not taking the opportunity to get some answers.

"Please." Adam nodded. "Ask me anything. But I think I already know what you're going to ask."

I wasn't surprised. Instead of vocalizing the question, I took a deep breath as Adam began to explain.

ADAM

Thirty-Seven Years Ago

I woke up before the sunrise. Truthfully, I'd hardly slept at all the night before. Or for the last few nights.

Not since I'd told Maureen about the opportunity to go to South Africa and work on the medical team.

It was my dream. Ever since my third year of optometry school when I'd first heard about the charity that went from village to village helping impoverished people by treating their eye infections, passing out old donated prescription glasses and manning eye health for people who would never normally have access to that kind of care, I'd known that it was exactly what I wanted to do when I graduated.

My entire life, I had wanted to help people in a way that would really make a difference. So when the opportunity to apply for the position came up, I jumped at it.

It had been a long shot. The program only took a few candidates every year. But I had to try because I couldn't imagine doing anything else.

That was, until I'd met Maureen.

In an instant, the moment I heard her sweet voice ordering a lemonade, I knew it was the only sound I ever wanted to hear again. And then, later, when I pulled her close on the dance floor and stared into her eyes, my heart knew it before I did.

I was lost to her.

When my Aunt Judy and Uncle Jack extended the invitation to spend the summer with them at the lake, I jumped at the offer. I was exhausted from spending the last six years at school. The last two especially had been intense with all the board exams and clinical work. I was overdue for a break and a few months to relax, have fun and figure out what I wanted to do now that I'd graduated. *If* I didn't get accepted into the program in South Africa.

I hadn't planned on meeting Maureen.

Not that I'd change the last few weeks for anything. They'd been some of the best of my entire life.

I replayed every moment with her as I slipped from my uncle's house and made my way through the quiet streets to the city dock so early in the morning, there were only a few people launching fishing boats. But otherwise, I had the dock to myself, which was exactly what I needed to think. I sat on the edge, pulled my shoes off, and dropped my feet into the cool water.

There were twelve hours until I was supposed to meet Maureen for dinner.

I dropped my head into my hands.

"Adam?"

I looked up slowly to see my Uncle Jack, my father's brother, standing next to me.

"I thought I might find you out here." He gestured with his head. "May I sit?"

I nodded and moved over a bit to make room on the edge.

"I didn't mean to wake you," I said. "I needed to think and…"

"You've got a big decision in front of you."

My aunt and uncle had been thrilled for me when my mother called with the news that a letter had arrived from the foundation. She'd read it to me over the phone, and Aunt Judy had pulled out a special bottle of wine that was dusty on the shelf to celebrate. I may not have seen them much since I was a kid, but they'd kept in touch, and both Uncle Jack and Aunt Judy knew exactly what this opportunity meant to me.

They also knew what Maureen meant to me.

"I don't know what to do."

My uncle was quiet for a moment before he spoke again. "Are you sure?"

"Sure about what?"

"That you don't know what to do," he said simply. "Because I think you might know more than you think you do."

I shook my head and stared at my foot in the water as I traced circles with my toe.

"Sometimes I find it helps to talk it out," Uncle Jack said. "And if you like, I can be a pretty good sounding board."

It couldn't hurt.

"The way I see it, there are a few potential outcomes and they're all impossible."

Jack nodded, so I continued.

"I could turn down the offer and stay here with Maureen."

My uncle raised one eyebrow.

It wasn't a question, but I shook my head. "We could be together, Uncle Jack. Maureen would go to school, and I could start up a practice. We would get married and have a family. Hell, maybe we could even spend our summers at the lake here? That wouldn't be too bad."

"It wouldn't."

The idea of having a life with Maureen made me smile. I could picture it. It would be a good life.

"You'd give up your dream for her?"

"Yes." I didn't hesitate.

"And Maureen would be okay with that?"

The smile fell from my face. "No." I'd always known the answer to that question, which was why I'd never really considered it an option before. She would never let me give up my dream for her. She loved me too much. And if for some reason she did, there would be disappointment in what I missed out on. In time, resentment might grow. "She would never let me give up my dream. Not even for her."

Jack nodded. "And what about her? You said you asked her to come with you."

I nodded. That was the best possible outcome, in my mind. Together, we could change the world and make a difference. It would be an amazing adventure.

"And what do you think she'll say?"

She loved me almost as much as I loved her. I knew I'd caught her off guard when I'd asked her about Africa with no warning, but I also knew Maureen. "I think she'll say yes."

"You do?" If my uncle was surprised, he didn't show it.

"I do." I lifted a foot and let it splash down into the water. "Maureen is a beautiful girl," I said with a smile. "But more than that, she's smart and passionate and stubborn. She won't give up on us. If I know her, she's probably spent the last few days making lists and researching and learning everything she can about Africa." I smiled at myself and shook my head a little in wonder. "She's incredible."

"Then what exactly is the problem?"

"The problem is…she'll say yes." I turned to look at my uncle, who immediately reached over and put an arm around my shoulders. He pulled me close, as if I were a small boy again. In my uncle's embrace, for the first time, I let myself cry because I knew what I had to do. I loved Maureen too much not to.

After a few minutes, I wiped my eyes and sat up straight. "I need you to do something for me, Uncle Jack."

MAUREEN

Present

"It was your Uncle Jack who dropped off the letter."

Adam nodded.

Even after so many years, I heard the emotion in his voice as he told me his story.

"I waited for you." My own voice cracked.

"I know."

I reached for his hand again. I hadn't realized I'd pulled away.

"I can't even begin to tell you how sorry I am for the way I left like that. But I don't regret my decision, Maureen."

I squeezed his hand, and the simple act of it made me want to cry.

"I was devastated, Adam." My voice was quiet, almost unrecognizable. "I didn't think I would survive it."

"But you did."

I looked up into his eyes. "I did," I said simply.

"And you understand?"

I nodded. "I do." I inhaled deeply. "I didn't at first," I admitted after a moment. "But in time, I did."

We sat in silence for a few minutes, simply looking into each other's eyes. "You have a family."

I nodded. "A beautiful family."

"I knew you would."

And that was why he'd done it. That was the entire reason he'd stood me up all those years ago. "Four sons and two sort-of daughters."

"Sort of?"

I laughed. "It's a long story."

"I'd love to hear it." Adam stroked the back of my hand with his thumb. "I'd love to hear all of it. And it turns out that I'm newly retired, and I have nothing but time."

Elise's words from earlier echoed in my head. *You always think you'll have time. That's a lie.*

"Adam, would you like to go dancing with me?"

"That's not what I was expecting you to say." He chuckled. "But, yes. Of course. I'd love to go dancing with you, Maureen. More than anything, I'd love to hear all about your life, dance the nights away with you, and drink lemonade on a dock, looking out at the lake. I know it's been decades, and there is much we don't know about each other. But like I said earlier, I would still know you anywhere. And the truth is, I knew when I made the decision to go to Africa that I was breaking your heart, and I went on to live my life knowing I had broken it. The least I can do now is to spend the rest of my days helping mend it as best I can. If you'll let me?"

I sucked in a breath.

"All those years ago, the timing wasn't right. We were on different paths."

I nodded in agreement as he spoke.

"I don't regret the way my life turned out, and I'm sure you don't either."

"I don't."

"But I do regret one thing."

"What's that?"

"Not looking for you earlier." Adam looked into my eyes. "I told myself that when I finally retired, I'd look you up and see…"

"If I was married?"

He nodded.

"I couldn't come to grips with it in my head," he said. "More than anything, I wanted you to be happily married and have a house full of children and grandchildren. But at the same time…" He dropped his head and gave it a shake before looking up again. "Truthfully and selfishly, I was terrified that you would be."

"I know," I said with a sad smile. That was never more true than now after I heard his version of how things went that summer. I'd always known why he left, but to hear it from his own mouth, after all this time, hit differently.

"I never stopped thinking about you, Maureen. Not for one day. You were it for me."

The idea that Adam had been alone for all these years struck me as terribly sad. "You never married?"

He shook his head. "There were women over the years. Some I was quite fond of."

"But?"

"None of them were you."

I sucked in a breath. "You don't mean that." I could see by the look on his face that he did.

"Your husband?"

"Ex."

"Ex-husband," he corrected himself. "He—"

"Wasn't you."

Chapter Ten

Present

THE BAND, the Lost Ridge Ramblers, was fun and upbeat.

We could have stayed at the restaurant and talked all night about the years we'd spent apart, filling in the blanks from the letters we'd written, but I had meant it when I'd asked him to dance. So we braved the storm that had lightened up considerably and made our way the short distance to the pub right next door to hit the dance floor.

It had been years since I'd danced with a man, but together, we fell easily into step. Just like everything about us, it felt like no time had passed since we'd been together.

The main difference was that so many years later, we were older and didn't have the same type of stamina to stay on the dance floor, despite our best efforts.

After a few songs and spins around the dance floor, Adam led me to a table in the corner. He excused himself to the bar and returned a few minutes later with two tall glasses.

"Is this lemonade?" I accepted the glass with a smile.

"Of course." Adam's boyish grin made me laugh. "It's our drink, after all."

I took a sip of the sweet liquid, closed my eyes, and savored the moment. "It's delicious," I said when I opened my eyes again. "Do you know that I haven't had a glass of lemonade since that summer?"

"What? But you had kids. How did you manage that?"

"I know it's ridiculous." I shrugged. "But I think it was self-preservation."

He reached for my hand. "I hate that we wasted so many years."

I hated it, too. But at the same time…

"I think things work out the way they're supposed to." I twined my fingers through his. Touching him felt so natural, I never wanted to let go. "If we'd reconnected any sooner, you might not have ever been able to start your charities and continue with all the good work you've done in Africa over the years. And I, well…I don't think I would have been in a place where I was ready for this. It's taken a lot of years of healing after Harold. Time I needed with my children and now with their partners, and the girls…" I let myself drift off as I thought of the last few years and everything that had changed both with my family and with myself. "It was important time," I said. "Because now I know without any uncertainty what I want and what I need. That's why I'm here."

A smile played at the corner of his lips. "And what is it that you need and want, Maureen?"

There were a million reasons I should slow down, proceed with caution, or play it cool, or even think about what my children might say about my relationship with a man I hadn't seen or spoken to in almost forty years.

But there was one, very important reason I shouldn't.

Tomorrow wasn't guaranteed. Time was finite, and we'd already let so much time go by.

"It might be crazy." I shook my head. "But I don't care." I took a breath. I'd already taken the biggest risk by getting on a plane mere days before Christmas and my son's wedding to meet with Adam; there was no bigger risk. Besides, judging by the way he looked at me, I was pretty certain there was no risk at all. "I want to be with you, Adam." My free hand flew to my mouth, and I chuckled in disbelief at my brazenness. It also emboldened me. "After all these years, I want to see what we could be together."

He'd begun to nod slowly while I spoke. "It wasn't our time then." Adam swallowed hard and took my other hand in his. "But I believe that it might just finally be our time now, Maureen."

"There's only one way to find out."

"I couldn't agree more." His hand cupped my cheek and when his lips touched mine, the room around us disappeared.

I was floating on air the next morning as I made my way down to the lobby of the inn. The night before, after we shared what had to be the very best kiss of my entire life, dancing was forgotten as we made our way back to the main building, and up to my room.

It had been so long since I had been with a man that I should have been nervous but with Adam, everything felt natural and *right*. It was as if no time had passed between us at all.

I'd fallen asleep in his arms, knowing that I was exactly where I belonged.

The storm had settled overnight, and the sun shined through the windows as I descended the steps into the busy lobby. Now that the storm had stopped, I assumed many people were trying to make arrangements to get home for the holidays. I bypassed the chaos and headed straight for the beverage station, to get a coffee while I waited for Adam to finish his shower.

I'd just poured myself a cup and was heading toward a bench by a window when Lucy Gibbons caught up with me.

"Mrs. McCormick." The woman wrung her hands and looked as if she might cry. "I'm so sorry about last night. I meant to find you and Mr. Lancaster to sort out the room situation. I looked for you in the restaurant and—"

"It's fine." I gave the woman the most reassuring smile I could. "Mr. Lancaster...ended up...well..." I shook my head and laughed a little at my ridiculous embarrassment. I was a grown woman, after all. "Well, he stayed with me last night."

"Oh. I..."

"It's fine, Lucy. But thank you for your concern. I do appreciate the attention to detail you all have."

The woman pulled back her shoulders and beamed with pride. "I'm glad it all worked out, Mrs. McCormick. Thank you for being so understanding." She glanced behind her toward the desk. "It's a bit chaotic here this morning, and along with the roads being closed for the next few days, we've had a bit of a situation come up. Please excuse me if I—"

"A few days?"

Lucy nodded seriously. "Oh yes. When a storm like this comes along, the roads are always closed for a few days as the plows get mobilized and..." Something across the room caught her attention, and she looked away.

"You're busy," I said. "I don't want to keep you."

"I will let you know just as soon as the roads get cleared. I am sorry."

"Don't be ridiculous. You can't do anything about the weather." I waved her away. "Don't worry about me at all. I've enjoyed my stay here very much. Go. Take care of whatever you need to."

Lucy made a few more apologies before finally leaving me and returning to the desk and no doubt a growing to-do list.

For a few minutes, I sipped my coffee in peace as I gazed out at the snowy landscape. The mountains of North Carolina were beautiful. Very different from the Rocky Mountains I was used to back home, but equally stunning. With everything outside covered in snow, I felt cozy and warm inside the inn.

Maybe a few more days trapped in the inn with Adam wouldn't be so bad. My face flushed with the memory of the night before.

Oh no. It wouldn't be bad at all.

Eventually, I'd have to go home, and to the real world. With the road closure, I'd be cutting it close for Cal's wedding, and Clara's first Christmas. But I'd make it.

And maybe I wouldn't have to go alone?

The thought was so unexpected that it shocked me momentarily. But only for a second, as I let myself think about what it would mean if I asked Adam to accompany me back to Cedar Springs and how perfect it would be.

"Excuse me."

Pulled out of my thoughts, I turned to see a woman with red-rimmed, puffy eyes standing behind me.

"I don't mean to interrupt," the woman said. "I'm sorry. I just—"

It was then that I noticed the bag in the woman's hands. The same bag I'd returned to the front desk the night before. "Susan?"

The woman nodded.

"I'm glad you got her crochet bag back. Elise mentioned how determined she was to finish a baby blanket." I smiled and my smile stretched across my face. "Such a lovely woman. I really enjoyed chatting with her last night and it looks like we all might be stranded—" A tear slid down Susan's cheek, and the smile fell from my face. "Is everything okay?"

"Yes. I mean…no." Susan shook her head. "I'm sorry. This is all so…"

"Sit." I waved to the empty seat next to her. "Please."

I waited until Susan was seated before I reached out and patted her hand. "If there's anything I can—"

"She's gone."

I froze. Something in Susan's voice told me what I needed to know. Still, I asked, "Gone? You mean—"

"She passed away in her sleep last night."

My hand flew to my mouth. "But…I was…" I couldn't formulate the thoughts I needed to. "She seemed just fine. We had such a lovely conversation last night."

Susan nodded. I gestured toward the front desk with my head. "They told me you sat with her most of the evening last night." Susan shook her head and chuckled a little bit. "I thought she was in bed. She told me…"

"She did mention that you'd be upset with her if you knew she was downstairs instead of in bed." I smiled a little, remembering the conversation I'd shared with the older woman the night before.

"I wanted her to rest," the other woman said with a sigh. "I should have known better to know that she wouldn't. She was so stubborn." A sob escaped my throat. "It feels wrong to speak about her in the past tense. She should…"

I waited while the other woman pulled herself together.

"She was sick," Susan said after a moment. "I don't imagine she told you that?"

I shook my head. "We talked about a lot of things. But she didn't mention that."

"She wouldn't have. Like I said, she was stubborn. She knew she didn't have a long time left, but she refused to do anything about it. I think she was ready."

I put my hand on Susan's arm. "To be with your mom."

Susan looked at me in surprise. "You did talk about a lot of things."

"We did," I said with a soft laugh. "It was an evening I'll never forget."

"Elise had that effect on people."

The two women sat in silence for a few minutes before Susan spoke again. "I don't know what I'm going to do with this." I lifted the crochet bag with the half-finished baby blanket in it. "I can't really give the baby half a blanket, now can I?"

I looked at the bag before letting my eyes drift toward the fireplace and the chair where Elise had sat all night, determinedly working on the project. "I know this might be a little odd." I turned back to Susan. "But would you let me finish it? It's been a long time since I've crocheted, but I know how important it was to her, and I'd be happy to finish it and send it to you when it's done. Kind of like a thank-you for the wisdom she imparted to me. I can't really explain it, but she really helped me yesterday, and I'd really like the opportunity to repay the favor."

Susan looked down at the bag in my lap and was silent for so long that I wondered whether I'd overstepped. When she looked up, there were tears in her eyes, but she was smiling. "I think that would be really nice. Thank you."

The women exchanged information and a hug before Susan handed me the crochet bag and left to take care of the details of Elise's passing.

A few minutes later, Adam appeared. He greeted me with a kiss on the cheek. "What's that?" He pointed to the bag in my lap.

I already knew what I wanted to happen next, but talking to Susan and hearing about Elise had only strengthened my resolution. "This is a reminder." I blinked slowly. "To not waste one more minute. Life is short, Adam."

He nodded in agreement, despite the look of confusion on his face.

"I don't want to waste one more day. It sounds like we might be trapped here for a few days, but when the roads clear..." I pulled my shoulders back, took a breath, and asked my questions. "Will you come back to Cedar Springs with me for the holidays? Cal gets married on Christmas Eve, and I know it might seem a bit fast and—"

"Of course." He stopped me and lifted my chin gently with two fingers. "I will go anywhere with you, Maureen. And no, it doesn't seem fast. It's been almost forty years. There's nothing fast about that. I said it before, and I'll say it again and again. It's always been you, Maureen. It will always be you."

Tears slipped down my cheeks, but I wasn't sad as I leaned forward and kissed the love of my life.

Epilogue

"YOU LOOK ABSOLUTELY GORGEOUS." I clasped my hands together and gushed over my soon-to-be daughter-in-law. "Milena, you are truly the most beautiful bride I've ever seen."

"You say that to all of the brides," Milena protested, but I didn't miss the pink glow on her cheeks.

"Maybe I do." I laughed. "There's just something about love that lights a woman up. And you, my dear, are positively radiant."

I gave the bride one last hug and, along with the other girls, left Milena in her father's very nervous hands—the poor man looked like he might pass out with the role of giving his daughter away—and we moved into the hallway.

Because it was such a small and private wedding, Cal and Milena had organized it at Mitch's big house on the lake. The same place Mitch had held his surprise wedding to Jade. It was very romantic, especially with the pine boughs and pops of red holly berries that had been draped on every open surface.

It might be a small wedding, but Cal had spared no expense.

"Speaking of women in love…" Chelsea slipped her arm through mine. She wiggled her eyebrows and laughed.

"Oh, definitely," Gwen added as she appeared on my other side. "You are glowing, Maureen."

I didn't bother trying to deny it. They were right; I was completely, head over heels in love with Adam.

"And don't worry about the boys." Jade lifted an eyebrow. "They'll come around."

The "boys" she referred to were Mitch and Ian.

Although most of my children and their partners had been very accepting and welcoming of Adam when I surprised them all the day before by returning to Cedar Springs with him after our extended stay at the Merry Falls Inn, my oldest two sons had been less thrilled, and they hadn't done an excellent job hiding it.

"They're just being protective," Chelsea added. "Trust me. Once they got over *who* I was, they took their big brother roles very seriously."

I chuckled. I knew all about when Chelsea had first come to town to stay with Ian and the growing pains they'd had. I also was well aware of how protective my two oldest could be with the women in their lives.

"Well, they better get used to it soon," I said as we reached the living room, where a few rows of chairs had been set up for the very few people who'd been invited. I scanned the small crowd and found Adam in the second row. "Because he's not going anywhere."

"Good." Gwen squeezed my shoulders. "I love seeing you so happy."

"We all do," Jade added. "But we better take our seats. I think it's supposed to start soon. I'll get the guys."

"Let me." I put my hand on my daughter-in-law's arm. "I'd like to say a few words to Cal first."

"Of course."

The women headed into the living room to take their seats, and I made my way to the kitchen, where the men were huddled around Cal.

I paused in the doorway, taking in the sight of all my sons together. There had been a time when I wouldn't have been able to imagine all of them like this, here in this place. Now, I couldn't imagine them being anywhere else. My heart swelled with love for all of them.

"I'm sorry to interrupt, boys."

"Mom." Declan turned around and saw me first. He held out an arm and beckoned me closer.

Happily, I joined my sons in their circle.

"We were just giving Cal some last-minute advice." Ian chuckled.

"Is that right? Odd, since only one of you has managed to get married so far."

"Boom!" Cal howled. "She's right, brothers. Get it together."

They all laughed, but I knew it was all in fun. All my sons were equally committed to the women in their life. Wedding ceremony or not.

"I do think we should place bets on who's next," Mitch said.

Declan let out a low whistle. "My bet's on Mom."

I froze, as did the room around me.

"What?" Ian shook his head. "No way."

"Why not?" Declan defended me. "When you know, you know. And anyone can see by looking at the two of them that they know."

Married?

The idea should have been ridiculous, considering we'd only *just* reconnected. But it didn't feel ridiculous at all.

"They just met, Dec," Ian protested. "You can't just marry off Mom."

I shook myself out of my thoughts and put a hand on each of my sons' arms. "We're not here to talk about my relationship. This is Cal's day." I gave them each a stern look. "The only relationship we're talking about is the most important one today." I focused on Cal and smiled softly. "I'm so proud of you, son."

He wrapped his arms around me and squeezed me tight. I worked hard to keep my tears at bay as I embraced my youngest.

"Thank you for everything, Mom. I mean it. Everything."

I sniffed and squeezed my eyes shut, losing the battle against the tears. I couldn't speak for fear that if I did, I'd start to sob.

"It's because of you that I am the man she deserves." He squeezed me again and stepped back.

It was only once he released me that I realized we were alone.

There were unshed tears shining in Cal's eyes, but he grinned from ear to ear.

"You are going to make an amazing husband, Cal. I really am so proud of you." I swallowed hard and waved my hand in an effort to ward off the tears. At least for a few more minutes.

"Will you walk with me?"

Taken aback, I was speechless for a moment. When Milena and Cal had decided on a small, intimate wedding, they'd agreed not to have any wedding party at all and do away with most of the formalities.

"I'd love nothing more."

Together, we walked down the small aisle to where the officiant was waiting for us. I gave Cal one last hug and kissed him on the cheek. "I love you, son."

"I love you, too, Mom. And for what it's worth, I think Declan's right. You'll be next," he added with a wink.

The ceremony was short and sweet, and absolutely perfect.

I didn't bother to hide my tears as my youngest son read his vows to the love of his life in what felt like the most romantic wedding I'd ever seen. Of course, I was sure I'd thought that about Mitch and Jade's wedding, and there was no doubt I'd feel the same about the rest of my children, too.

At some point during the ceremony, Adam slipped his hand into mine and squeezed gently for support. When the ceremony was over, we walked down the short aisle together, hand in hand.

"That was beautiful," Adam whispered to me. "They are so obviously very much in love."

"They are." I smiled up at him. "I'm so happy for him. For all my children," I added.

"And for yourself?"

The question was unexpected, but it didn't take me off guard. I'd spent a lifetime coming to terms with my feelings. I didn't hesitate with my answers. "Oh yes, definitely for myself, too."

We didn't have time to discuss what that might mean any further, as we quickly got swept up in wedding festivities. I was kept busy with photos and all the other duties for the mother of the groom while Adam was left to his own devices.

Not that I was worried at all about him or how he'd fit in. In the very short time since we'd been back in Cedar Springs, Adam had slipped easily into my life. It was probably way too soon to make such declarations, but I had a sense about these things and it didn't take an expert at relationships to see how easily he got along with everyone.

Even Mitch and Ian.

My eldest sons were putting up a tough front with some sort of misguided need to protect me, but it was clear to see that they, too, could see what a good guy Adam was.

It wasn't until much later, after the dinner and the toasts, when I found myself with some uninterrupted time with Adam on the makeshift dance floor.

"Thank you," Adam whispered into my ear after spinning me easily and pulling me back into his arms.

"For what?"

"For including me in your life like this. Today was a very special day."

I felt the warmth through my body and down to my toes. "It really was. Cal and Milena are—"

"I don't mean just the wedding," he interrupted me gently. "Although it truly was the perfect celebration of love."

I gave him a confused look, but he only chuckled.

"Today was extra special for me because seeing you with your family and how much you all love each other is truly remarkable. *You* have created something absolutely wonderful here, Maureen. You are truly wonderful." He guided us into a quieter corner of the dance floor and held me close. "Allowing me to be part of this, is…well, there really are no words except for, thank you."

I let my hand slide down his cheek and rest there as I gazed into his eyes, which were both familiar and completely new to me. "Adam, I can't imagine today without you here. You fit in so well and…" I inhaled deeply. What I had to say next scared me, but scared or not, I refused to waste any more time. "I'd like you to stay."

"Well, that works out then." His smile lit up his face.

"It does?"

"It sure does." He lowered his head so his lips were only

inches from mine. "Because I don't plan on leaving you again anytime soon."

My heart melted with his words. I could feel his love right through to my core. I closed my eyes and leaned forward into a kiss.

"May I cut in?" Ian's arrival jolted us apart moments before our lips could touch.

I looked at my eldest son and back at Adam. "I don't know if—"

"Of course." Adam graciously held out my hand to Ian, gave me a wink, and stepped back.

Seconds later, Ian swept me up into an easy dance.

"Listen, Ian. I know you're not excited about me dating, and you think that maybe I'm moving too quickly. But Adam and I—"

"Mom." He stopped me with a grin. "It's okay."

Of all the things I'd expected him to say, *okay* wasn't one of them. "What do you mean?" I eyed him suspiciously.

"I wanted to tell you that I was wrong. I'm sorry."

Completely flabbergasted, I stumbled over my feet and stopped dancing altogether to stop and stare at my son. "I'm sorry, you were what?"

He laughed. "I was wrong." Ian shrugged. "About Adam. About the two of you. I'm sorry."

"I don't know what to say."

"Don't say anything." He took my hand again and once more started moving through the dance floor. "I just want you to be happy, Mom."

"Thank you." I blinked back tears. "Can I ask you what made you change your mind? I mean, I know this must seem fast to all of you. But it's been a lifetime for Adam and me and—"

"That's just it, Mom." Ian looked down into my eyes. "I

was so caught up in protecting you that I couldn't see it until it was pointed out to me."

I tilted my head in question but let him continue.

"Gwen made me see and once she did, it was clear."

"What was clear?"

"The way he looks at you, Mom." Ian shook his head in wonder. "I'm not an expert in love or relationships or anything like that, but I can see it, too. He loves you, Mom."

A tear slipped down my cheek, but I didn't move to wipe it away. "And I love him."

"I know, Mom." His smile was genuine, and it filled my heart to know I'd raised such a caring and loving man. "I'm still going to be protective of you." He tried to look stern. "But the more I get to know him, the more I can see what a good guy he is. And we all just want you to be happy. You deserve it."

I hadn't noticed that while Ian was talking, he'd guided me back to where we'd left Adam until Ian stepped back and offered him my arm. "Be good to her."

"Always." Adam looked first at Ian, and then to me as he took me in his arms.

It was just the two of us when Adam looked into my eyes. "I love you, Maureen. It's always been you."

Through all the years, my marriage, raising children and my divorce, I had always known the truth of my heart, too. "It's always been you, Adam. And finally, it's our moment."

"Forever."

I laughed. "Our forever moment."

———

I hope you enjoyed the McCormick family.

If you love small town romance that revolves around

a big, loving family as much as I do, you'll love the brand new Trickle Creek series and the Carlson family.

These stories are heartwarming, full of love and of course a happy ever after!

Read an excerpt of Never Let Me Go next...

Never Let Me Go

Please enjoy this excerpt of Never Let Me Go

CHASE

WHEN I PULLED open the door to the Bean Bag, I was greeted with the same familiar combination of jingling and clacking from the old bells that had hung above the glass door for years. The sound, paired with the rich, overpowering scent of freshly roasted coffee beans that hit me the second I stepped inside, was exactly as I remembered it.

I paused, keeping the door open to the stifling late-summer heat a little longer than necessary, my gaze lifting to the bells as I drew in a deep breath.

Some things never changed.

Then again, I thought as I looked past the doorway to the bustling plaza outside—crammed with tourists and the occasional local brave enough to wade into the chaos—some things really had.

The last time I'd been home in Trickle Creek, the idea of tourism had barely taken root. The golf course was still new, the only motel in town was a beat-up roadside relic, and no one had even thought of turning homes into vacation rentals— let alone building entire condo complexes for tourists.

But they had come.

And judging by the no-vacancy signs and out-of-province license plates crowding the streets, a lot of them had come.

I shook my head, closing the door behind me, and turned toward the café's interior. If I thought it was busy outside, it was even worse inside. Almost every table was full. A few people milled about by the doorway, either coming or going.

I wove my way through the tightly packed tables and found an empty seat at the counter near the coffee station. It would have to do. The noise and chaos suited me, honestly—a sharp contrast to the somber quiet of the scene I'd just left.

Not that a funeral could ever be anything else.

Still, somehow, I'd expected my father's to feel…different.

Actually, if I were being honest, I didn't really know what I'd expected. I hadn't given it much thought.

I was here out of duty—nothing more—for the man who'd put a roof over my head and given me his name when he married my mother. Michael Carlson might have been my stepfather, but he was the only father I'd ever known.

That didn't mean I'd ever really known him.

For as long as I could remember, I'd felt like an extra piece that didn't quite fit. An afterthought that came with the package when he'd married my mom.

For some reason I could never quite figure out, my sister Charli, two years younger, had always been the one to hold a special place in his life. Not me. Never me. Especially not after Mom died when I was twelve.

That was when I'd asked—no, insisted—on going to boarding school. I'd been just shy of thirteen when I left my sister, Charli, and my half-siblings—Asher, Craig, and Kat—behind.

There'd been visits after that, of course. Holidays. A few summers. But it didn't take long to realize that my presence hadn't been missed. And before I knew it, even those visits stopped altogether.

It had been nearly fifteen years since I'd last been back.

Maybe that was why I felt so out of place now. Why everything felt both familiar and foreign all at once.

And why I hadn't stuck around after the service.

I needed a few minutes alone—and a strong cup of coffee—before the will reading.

Coffee.

Right.

I glanced around for the waitress, but she hadn't come by yet to take my order. Her back was turned to me as she scribbled furiously in her notepad, trying to wrangle a table of six. A bell rang from the kitchen, signaling another order was up, but she didn't move. It looked like she was the only one working the busy cafe.

Shit. I didn't have time to wait for my caffeine fix.

I slipped off the stool and made my way behind the counter, where a fresh pot had just finished brewing. Casually, I filled a mug for myself. I was about to put the pot back when I noticed the guy sitting next to me needed a refill. So did the woman on his other side.

Before I knew it, I was refilling mugs—one, then another, then another. When a nearby table waved me over, I just shrugged and went. Might as well.

A small smile tugged at my mouth as I made the rounds. For the first time all day, I felt something that wasn't heavy. I made small talk, offered refills, moved from table to table and made easy conversation with the customers.

I was about to pour another cup when a small hand wrapped around my arm.

"What do you think you're doing?"

I turned.

The waitress stood behind me. A pretty brunette, hair clipped back with a couple of pencils shoved into the top. No makeup. Tired eyes. But even with the dark smudges of exhaustion shadowing her face, there was something about her. Cute, in a girl-next-door kind of way. Familiar somehow, though I couldn't place her.

Not that that was surprising. I'd grown up here. Faces blurred together.

I held up the coffeepot and offered a small grin. "Pouring coffee," I said, nodding toward the table that was still waiting. "Obviously."

Her expression didn't soften. "You need to stop. You don't work here."

"It doesn't mean I can't help." I surprised myself with how much I even cared. All I'd wanted was a cup for myself—and it was probably already getting cold at the counter. "You seemed a little—"

"I've got it." She snatched the pot gently from my hand and moved toward the table.

Then, after a pause, she looked back. "Thanks for helping."

That small acknowledgment brought my smile back. "Anytime."

I nodded toward my seat at the counter, holding her gaze for a beat before sitting down again.

I wrapped my hands around the warm mug, letting the steam rise against my face as I finally took a long sip. Strong, hot, and bitter—just the way I liked it. The noise around me swelled again, the kind of sound that filled all the quiet places inside a person, and I found myself almost grateful for it.

I didn't want to think about the service. Or the look on my siblings' faces when the officiant mentioned family. We'd all been standing shoulder to shoulder, but I'd never felt further away from them.

Family.

That word had always carried more weight than warmth for me.

The bell above the door jingled again, another gust of hot air sweeping in. Voices rose and fell around me, laughter mixing with clinking cups. Trickle Creek had changed, that was for sure. But even with the crowds, it still felt like a small town—the kind of place where everyone knew everyone else's story.

Everyone except mine.

ANNIE

By the time I dropped the last of the lunch rush orders and circled back behind the counter, my legs were shaking. I'd been running on autopilot for hours. I started another pot of coffee, praying it would brew fast enough to keep up with the demand, and maybe give me a second to breathe.

If I was lucky, I might even get a sip of water before the next round hit.

Monica had called in sick again, and of course there was no one else to cover the shift. Everyone in town was short-staffed these days, and that meant I got to handle the entire lunch rush solo—for the second time this week.

To say I was exhausted was an understatement. I was so tired I could hardly remember what day it was. Not that it mattered much. My days all blurred together lately—work at the Bean Bag, then change into cleaning clothes and hit my list of vacation rentals before picking up—

"Hey."

The deep, friendly voice behind me made me turn. "I could use a refresh," he said, holding up his mug, "but I don't want to overstep."

It was the man from earlier, the one who'd decided to play waiter when I was drowning.

Up close, he was even more noticeable. Broad shoulders, dark navy suit, crisp white shirt. Totally out of place here in the mountain town of Trickle Creek. We were known for the world-class golf courses that dotted the valley, a vast network of hiking and mountain biking trails and of course, one of the best ski resorts in the Rockies, once the snow flew.

Where most guys wore golf polos or hiking gear. The suit made him stand out, but so did the quiet confidence behind it.

"Sorry," I said, grabbing the fresh pot that had just finished brewing. "I was waiting for a new one." I managed a small wink as I poured.

His smile reached his blue eyes, bright and steady. Handsome, I realized, in a way that was unfair to the rest of us who hadn't slept properly in weeks.

He was definitely a tourist. I hadn't seen him before, and after living here my whole life, I knew almost everyone. Which meant: off-limits. I had one rule—no tourists.

No flings, no free drinks, no bad ideas.

I'd watched too many women in this town fall for visiting golfers looking for a good time aay from their wives and lives for a few nights. Some of the local women used the opportunity for free drinks and a little entertainment, but there were a few who took it a bit further. The men who promised the world and left behind heartbreak—or babies. My sister was proof enough of that.

I'd learned enough from watching my big sister to know what I didn't want from my life. Now I just needed to figure out what I did want.

"Thanks, Annie," he said.

I blinked. "You're welcome. How do you know my name?"

He nodded toward my chest, amusement flickering. "It's on your name tag."

Right. "Good point." I couldn't help but laugh. "You assumed it wasn't an alias?"

"Seemed like a safe bet."

His easy humor made me smile despite myself. I leaned back against the counter for a moment, just catching my breath. "So, what brings you to town? You don't look like you're here to golf —or mountain bike—or fish. Unless you're hiking in that suit."

"I'm here for a funeral."

"Oh." My stomach dropped. "I'm so sorry, I didn't—"

He waved it off. "Don't be. My father and I weren't close."

He took a sip of coffee, but something about the way he said it made me pause. I studied his face, and the puzzle pieces finally clicked.

"Chase Carlson?" I asked.

He almost choked on his drink but caught himself quickly, setting the cup down with practiced control. "Do I know you?"

"Yes—well, not really." I winced. "You did, sort of.

His brow lifted, eyes narrowing slightly in amusement.

"I used to know you," I said, cheeks heating. "I'm Annie."

He looked pointedly at my name tag again, and I straightened automatically. "Annie Darling," I clarified. "I'm friends with your sister, Kat. I was probably about six when you left town. We grew up together."

"I see." He nodded slowly. "Sorry to say I had a lot going on back then. Not much time for paying attention." Then he extended his hand, and something about the simple gesture made my heart jump. "Let's start over. Nice to meet you, Annie Darling. I'm Chase Carlson."

When our hands met, warmth shot through me so fast it made my breath catch.

Was he always this handsome? No. He was just a kid then. So was I.

"I'm sorry about your—" I started.

He cut me off gently. "Please. Save that for Kat. Like I said, we weren't close."

I nodded, remembering all the times Kat had mentioned him—how her oldest brother had practically vanished from their lives. She talked about him less and less over the years, until he became more of a story than a person.

"Well, how long are you in town for, Chase?" I asked, trying not to sound as curious as I felt. Something about him made me want to forget about all my responsibilities. And for the briefest moment, I did.

He opened his mouth, but I held up a finger. "Hold that thought." I grabbed my notepad. "Table three's ready to pay, and table six needs water refills—and no, you can't help," I added quickly when he half stood from his stool. "Pretty sure I'll get fired if I let customers do my job."

He chuckled, the sound low and easy. "Fair enough. But I do need to get going." He glanced at his wristwatch—an old-fashioned one, not digital. Somehow, that fit him perfectly.

"I've got this thing," he said, a brief shadow crossing his expression before he looked back at me. "But to answer your question, I'll be in town a few days. Maybe we can grab a drink or something?"

For a second, I forgot how to breathe. "A drink?"

He smiled, warm and devastating. "I'll ask Kat for your number."

Before I could respond, he tossed some money on the

counter and gave me one last grin. "Nice to properly meet you, Annie."

And then he was gone—leaving me staring after him, heart thudding, wondering what the hell had just happened. Because it had been a very, very long time since anyone had made me feel like that.

Read the rest of Never Let Me Go NOW!

About the Author

Elena Aitken is a USA Today Bestselling Author of more than sixty romance and women's fiction novels. The mother of grown-up twins, Elena now lives with her very own mountain man and two dogs in the heart of the very mountains she writes about. She can often be found with her toes in the lake and a glass of wine in her hand, dreaming up her next book and working on her own happily ever after.

To learn more about Elena:
www.elenaaitken.com
elena@elenaaitken.com